THE TURNING

THE TURNING

Shannaaya Chopra

HarperCollins *Publishers* India

First published in India by HarperCollins *Publishers* 2025
HarperCollins *Publishers* India, Cyber City,
Building 10-A, Gurugram, Haryana – 122002, India
www.harpercollins.co.in

2 4 6 8 10 9 7 5 3 1

E-ISBN: 978-93-6989-819-0
P-ISBN: 978-93-6989-383-6
HB-ISBN: 978-93-7307-881-6

Covert design, art and inside illustrations by Omung Kumar

Typeset in 11.5/15.7 Baskerville Pro
by HarperCollins *Publishers* India Pvt. Ltd

Printed and bound at
Manipal Technologies Limited, Manipal

MIX
Paper | Supporting responsible forestry
FSC
www.fsc.org
FSC™ C043100

This book is produced from independently certified FSC® paper to ensure responsible forest management.

HarperCollins *Publishers*, Macken House, 39/40 Mayor Street Upper,
Dublin 1, D01 C9W8, Ireland

To my little sister

Tiny, I love you more than you can ever imagine

Prologue

CRISP BLACK SHOES stepped across puddles, causing ripples where the surfaces made contact.

The small, narrow alleyway was replete with puddles, and the brown brick walls rising on both sides were covered in wrinkled, dusty posters, weathered and torn, claw marks slashing across their grimy surface. A strange smell lingered in the air.

The wearer of the shoes was a tall, lean man. A massive black coat swished at his feet as he strode along. His silent demeanour seemed somehow intimidating. A flicker of fondness flashed over his face as his red eyes glanced up at the shining moon overhead.

He halted at an abandoned shoe shop, pushed open the rust-sprinkled door and walked through.

The little man inside the store flinched at the creak of the door. He was a stark contrast to the visitor. His shrivelled palms subconsciously extracted themselves from his pockets and he ran his fingers through his dark, matted hair. Strings hung off his ratty grey pants, which were otherwise covered in bulging pockets.

"Is it done, then?" the man in the coat asked, his eyes glittering with excitement.

"Yes," he replied, suddenly standing proudly in his shorter form and straightening his hunched back. He stretched his arms and neck, creating similar cracking sounds to the door that supposedly scared him a minute ago.

"And they don't know?"

"Of course not, Dmitry." He grinned, his eyes replicating the evil glint. "Do you think I am an imbecile?"

The pale visitor laughed and said, "Come here, William." He embraced him in a brotherly manner, his palm thumping his back multiple times.

William Farber pulled out a small green box from one of his many pockets.

The smile on the other man's face was cruel and cold. "Then our mission is officially in action, Farber," he said in a soft, commanding voice. They looked at each other and smirked.

As the man in black left the room, he looked up at the moon's unflinching stare.

"Another month, Kiara Sharma," he whispered to no one in particular. "Another month."

PART 1

1

NOT VERY FAR away, Kiara Sharma awoke on Friday morning with her head pounding to a loud, shrill noise.

She groggily glared at her ringing alarm clock. It was only her first week of school, and most of her friends were still out travelling. The good news, she reminded herself, was that it was the last day of school before the weekend, and that there were only a few weeks to her eighteenth birthday. The bad news was that she had to go through an entire six hours of school before she could enjoy two days of absolute freedom.

It took every ounce of her willpower to get out of bed that morning. She was quickly in and out of the shower and dressed. Pulling her hair back and tying it, she ran towards the kitchen, where a basket of fresh apples was the first thing she saw. Grabbing one, she kissed her father on the cheek. "You'll miss your train!" he called as she rushed out.

Kiara shuffled through her coin purse hastily, extracting change to pay for her auto ride. The local train was almost in motion when she jumped on. It was a fifteen-minute ride to school, so Kiara took her time sinking her teeth into that apple, her stomach growling furiously, and stared out of the window at the city she had called home ever since she was born.

The hustle and bustle of Mumbai was one of the reasons she loved the place so much. Everyone around her had something to do, somewhere to go. From the street vendors loudly proclaiming their discounted prices to the beaches to the polished 5-star hotels, Mumbai was, and had always been, home.

Upon reaching Santacruz station, Kiara got off and assessed herself in the glass wall of a grocery store. She was tall, with a lush waterfall of black hair cascading down her back, striking against her copper skin. Huge brown eyes stared back at her through the glass.

Kiara's eyes flew to her watch. For once, she was on time. She ran her hand over the scar on her wrist that she had had since she was two. Her father had told her that her late dog, Bailey, had scratched her there. A week after that, her mother had died.

Out of habit, her fingers made their way to the locket at her neck. It hung off a delicate silver chain. The pendant was a simple silver locket with a tiny blue gem in the centre. The locket looked like it could be pried open, and Kiara was curious to know what was inside, but her many attempts to open it had been unsuccessful. Only once it looked near broken had she decided to give up. It was the last piece of her mother she had left, and she had no intention of ever breaking it or taking it off.

She now walked into the school building, looking around for familiar faces. After about a minute of searching through the seemingly endless sea of students did she finally spot him—Krish Oberoi, her best friend. He was two years older than her, tall, muscular, with curly hair and a welcoming smile. She had often noticed girls throwing her envious glances when she was with him, or giggling every time he walked by. Kiara had always seen him as a brother, and he had always protected her like a little sister.

Krish had been travelling all summer and had just returned. He was now pacing back and forth, frowning, talking in a hushed voice with someone on the phone. "Krish!" Kiara called and his eyes met hers. He hastily whispered something and put down the phone, his worried expression clearing. As he walked towards her, his face broke out into a goofy grin.

Kiara knew she would never admit just how much she had missed him, but as he made his way over, she felt complete again, the hollow space in her heart filling up at the sight of him. He enveloped her in a giant bear hug, and she breathed in the familiar scent of his cinnamon soap. He buried his face into her shoulder, and Kiara felt her throat tighten with emotion. They broke apart after a moment, both still grinning.

"Hey," he said, his voice shaking slightly.

"Hey," Kiara put her hand on his arm. His shoulders relaxed. "What was that call about?"

"No, that–it was nothing," he said, his tone falsely cheery. She didn't want to push him; he would talk to her when he was ready.

"So, how's it going, Kie?" He never called her Kiara. Then suddenly his smile dissolved, and he gave her a concerned glance.

"Kie? What's wrong?" he asked.

Without even realizing it, she had clasped her mother's locket, the way she did every time she was anxious. "Think I forgot to do some homework," she lied. He raised his eyebrows. "I'm fine, seriously!" she added, but he didn't look convinced. She was saved from answering any other questions by the bell.

"Hey, I should probably go. Don't want to be late for the first class. But see you after school with everyone?" He was still scowling at her, but nodded.

Kiara made her way to art class and forgot her unease as she stepped into the studio. She barely heard the teacher telling them something about fantastical creatures. Soon her pencil moved as if of its own accord. She got lost in the art, in creating a new world, her world. The brush made its way over the white surface, leaving elegant strokes in its wake. Her palette was overflowing with shades of red and brown. Soon her clothes were splattered with colour. She hummed as her composition came to life.

"Oh, Kiara, what happened?" exclaimed her teacher. Kiara gave a start and glared at the teacher before realizing where she was. She gave the aghast teacher a smile and murmured an apology. "It's a stunning piece," Miss Shruti continued, "but your impatience and temper will get you nowhere."

Kiara stepped back to look at her work and cursed in frustration. A massive brown wolf watched her from the canvas, its shining red eyes wicked, its thick fur matted with blood. Having run out of black paint, Kiara had crushed the tube between her fingers, causing massive black splotches to appear across her artwork. She tilted her head; the wolf looked strangely familiar ...

The bell rang, promptly dismissing her line of thought. Kiara handed over the assignment to the teacher and swiftly moved out of the classroom, her head exploding with all the thoughts she'd buried earlier. She shook her head, as if trying to physically force them out, and cursed her overactive brain as she made her way through the school.

"Hey, Kie!" someone called. She turned around to see Advik standing a few steps away from her, with Rishika, Hritik and Krish. She walked up to them. Soon, Aisha joined the little group. Krish counted them and announced, "Six," solemnly. They broke into chatter, exchanging hugs and stories.

"What happened to you?" Rishika was asking Advik.

Advik had his palm over his left eye, and was wincing and cursing softly. "I couldn't see the nozzle of my deodorant, but I sprayed it anyway, and now I can't see anything," he complained. Kiara choked on her water.

Hritik was looking glum. "What's the matter, love?" Aisha asked him, her eyes filled with affection.

"I got my algebra results back," he admitted. Aisha let out a peal of laughter, a beautiful, free sound.

Krish made his way over to Kiara. "What's going on here?"

"Advik is yet to graduate the second grade," she reported.

Krish looked half-puzzled, half-amused. "What's up with them?" Kiara asked, pointing at Aisha and Hritik. Krish rolled his eyes. "They can't keep their hands off each other." Hritik's sibling felt disgusted looking at them.

"Can you blame her? She is his sister."

Krish nodded, amusement flickering across his face. Before long, Kiara, Krish, Advik, Rishika, Hritik and Aisha had slung their arms around each other's shoulders, and were laughing and teasing one another. Kiara felt her heart flutter with contentment. They made their way to an abandoned construction site a few minutes' walk from their school. The sweltering sun was merciless, but the evening flashed by in a blur of laughter, stories and rumours, and they felt happiness at being together after so long (also Rish's disgust at Aisha and Hritik).

When they decided to leave for home, they found Rishika curled up in a corner, fast asleep. Advik took his water bottle out of his backpack. Hritik looked like he wanted to protest, but thought better of it. He watched along with the rest of the crew as Advik cautiously stepped towards Hritik's little sister and uncapped the bottle over her head.

Her shriek kept Kiara smiling and in a good mood as she ate dinner with her father later that evening.

"So, how was school?"

Manohar Sharma was a simple man who lived an ordinary and honest life. He was copper-skinned and short-haired. Kiara's smile and crooked teeth were identical to his. He had never wanted to remarry after his wife's death, and even though years had passed since the tragedy, his eyes still held a haunted gleam.

"Kia?"

"Everything's great, Dad," she said, and a small, rare smile bloomed on her father's face. She felt a wave of satisfaction knowing she was the reason for it.

They finished their meal over easy, light conversation. Kiara felt her fingers itch to reach for her locket, and told her father it had been a long day, that she needed to sleep. His eyes were troubled and concerned as he kissed her forehead.

Kiara ran up to her room, locked the door and buried her face into her trembling hands.

A month to go. A month.

It seemed like too much time to wait, and too little time to prepare herself. Kiara had never believed her mother's untimely death was an accident. Months after Anjali Sharma's passing, Manohar had plucked up enough courage to look through his deceased wife's belongings. He had found a letter to be given to Kiara on her eighteenth birthday, a letter for himself and a chain with her locket. Kiara hadn't said anything at the time, but had always felt as if her mother had been anticipating her death, even preparing for it.

She was just a few weeks away from reading the letter, and was absolutely terrified. Her gut had always told her that the letter was bad news, and she'd told herself she was being cynical. But she knew she wasn't ready to face whatever pent-up emotions the letter would bring to the surface. Clasping her locket, she whispered, "What happened to you? What were you hiding, Mom?"

At that moment, the wind howled, as if in reply.

2

KRISH FORCED HIS lips into a smile as he approached his best friend.

Kiara was having a heated, intense discussion with Aisha in the school corridor. Her arms flailed about as she made wild gestures and exaggerated statements. Aisha looked as if it was taking her all her willpower to not burst out laughing.

"—did not just do that!" Kiara was saying.

"Well ..." Aisha shrugged.

Kiara caught sight of Krish and her face brightened.

"Listen to this," she said to him as he took a seat, pointing an accusing finger at Aisha. "She flirted her way out of a history assignment. I didn't finish mine either, and I have to do four extra projects!"

Krish forced out a chuckle. He looked at Aisha. "You," he said, "have got to teach me how to do that, though I doubt I'd need your help. Mr Kartik and I have always got along very well."

Aisha giggled.

"Could I steal Sharma here for a second?"

"Sure."

"What are you—" Kiara started once he'd pulled her away.

"The DATE!" he blurted out so loudly a passerby spilled his

juice on his pants. "Sorry, man," Krish muttered, flushing, to the other boy.

Kiara restrained a grin. "The, uh, the date?"

Krish whipped out his phone. "It's September fourth. You know, the day before your birthday." *The day before I have to–* he stopped himself short.

"O-kay. And?"

Krish's fingers danced along the keyboard on his phone. Kiara's own phone buzzed.

"Meet me here. 11:50 tonight," he said. "And wear something nice."

Her eyes lit up. "Are the others coming?"

He didn't want to lie to her more than he had to, so he settled on a tentative and suspenseful, "You'll see." Then he smiled and added, "Enjoy project-making." He squeezed her shoulder and walked away.

Krish's day seemed to drag on for ages. He didn't know what to do with himself once home. He tried to sleep to pass the time, but kept twisting and turning in bed, his back drenched with perspiration and hands shaking to the point where he couldn't even hold up a water bottle. He tried telling himself his hunch would probably not pan out, that nothing would go wrong, but this only made him more anxious. He knew he was lying to himself.

He fumbled about for his phone. Amara picked up on the third ring.

"Hey," she said. The tension in his muscles relaxed slightly at her soothing voice.

He opened his mouth to answer, but couldn't seem to force the words out. Instead, she listened to his heavy breathing in silence for the next two hours.

It's going to happen anyway, Krish thought, *you should do your best to at least make it easier for her.*

Finally, night fell. He gulped in a lungful of air and hastily threw on some clothes.

"Kie's birthday's tomorrow, right?" his mother asked him. He nodded. "Bring her home tomorrow. I haven't seen her in so long."

He grimaced. Seeing the troubled look on his face, she tried to force food into his mouth.

He smiled fondly at her. "I'm okay, Mumma. See you."

He was too nervous to drive, so he decided to take a long walk in the fresh air, since they were meeting outside a café only a few minutes from his place. A glance at his watch told him she would be there any minute now. Before he could re-enter his panicked spiral, he saw a sliver of brown hair.

"Kiara!" he breathed. "You look incredible."

"I know, thank you."

She wore a simple emerald green dress with black boots. Her hair was down, rippling down her back in waves. Her silver pendant hung around her neck as always, shimmering in the dim light. A simple purse hung on her shoulder. She wore close to no makeup, and Krish thought she didn't even need the little that she did. She was, and had always been, beautiful. Krish felt a surge of protectiveness towards her. He swore to himself he would do anything to make sure she was alright.

But he couldn't let her know what was going on just yet. He tried to act nonchalant. Putting on a smile, he went over to her. Apparently, he was not as good an actor as he thought, as Kiara scowled at him and asked what was wrong.

"It's nothing, Sharma," he said, making sure to put on his most convincing voice. "Follow me." He led her to an old, abandoned garage not far from the café.

He checked his watch. *11:57. Whatever happens, don't screw this up.*

Taking a blindfold out of his pocket, he told Kiara she could only go in with it on.

"Really?" she sighed, but went along with it anyway. *11:59.*

He led Kiara into the basement and took the chain out of his pocket, then quickly used it to bind her hands to the metal pole in the middle of the room as he had been taught.

Thirty seconds to go.

He remembered her necklace was made of silver, and quickly took it off to prevent it from hurting her, covering his fingers with the hem of his shirt as he did so, and then proceeded to take off her bag, watch and shoes.

"Hey, Krish, what's going on?"

"Nothing, Sharma. Just relax and trust me, okay?"

"Okay."

The scene might have looked sketchy to an outsider, but she trusted him completely, her tone implying as much. Krish felt a sharp stab of guilt. Since when had he become such a good liar? Since when had lying to his best friend come so naturally to him?

Ten seconds left.

Krish stepped back, drew a silver dagger from his belt and counted down the time to midnight in his head, dreading every passing second.

Five.

Four.

Three.

Two.

One.

It was happening.

3

KIARA HAD STARTED feeling uneasy the moment Krish put the blindfold on her.

Her discomfort only grew as he proceeded to rid her of her bag, watch, shoes and necklace. He'd told her everything was okay, and she believed him. She knew he'd never lie to her.

It must be twelve, she thought and waited for the blindfold to be taken off, for her friends to emerge from the shadows and scream, "Happy Birthday!"

Instead, she felt her body changing. She felt herself expanding and heard her dress ripping into shreds. Her fingers and toes felt suddenly rough. She struggled frantically against the chains. What was happening? Had she been drugged? Surely she was hallucinating. This could not be real.

Her body grew ... *softer*? She ran her coarse hands down her body and felt fur. She tried to call out for Krish, but her lips parted as her mouth swelled, her teeth becoming sharper and longer. They dug into her leathery lips. Her eyes flew open as the blindfold fell off against her will. She didn't want to see this–this *monster*–she felt herself turn into.

Kiara's vision was sharper, stronger. Trembling paws had replaced her hands. Her nails had elongated into long, grotesque claws. She wanted to let out a frustrated scream, but emitted a low growl instead.

Then, just as suddenly as it had arrived, her confusion vanished. She wasn't horrified or lost anymore, for one emotion took over, erasing every other feeling and thought.

Rage.

She could feel her mind slipping away as her head turned to her best friend. She tugged on the chains, and they rattled as they fell to the floor in pieces.

The last thing she heard was a beep and Krish's voice saying, "I was right. I need backup." He sounded panicked. Then came the darkness.

Kiara's head was pounding. Her limbs felt sore. She forced her eyes open. Instantly, her vision blurred. Biting back a gasp of pain, she tried to flex her fingers, her palms a canvas of dirt and grime. She winced even when she stretched her shoulders. She touched her right shoulder, and her fingers came away red.

Kiara started to sit up and let the blanket around her slip, but let out a horrified squeal as she realized her clothes were gone. She hugged the sorry excuse of a blanket tighter around herself.

She looked around. The dank, dull basement looked the same as it had before, eerily quiet and completely empty, save for a few silver pillars and poles, one with bloody chains tangled around its base ...

Her hand went to her throat out of habit, but her mother's locket was no longer there. She remembered very little of her birthday eve; the uncomfortable feel of heavy chains around her wrists, holding her down; Krish's voice; some kind of–she gasped as a sudden flashback hit her.

She had felt herself turning into this *thing*, a furry thing, with claws and a snout and–*Oh, shut up*, she thought, *you're being absurd.*

Am I, though? Am I?

"Kiara?" It was Krish. Dried tears traced his dirt-covered face. His eyes were bloodshot.

"Krish? Are you–are you okay?"

An anguished chuckle left his lips. "Of course," he whispered, shaking his head. "Of course, you'd first ask if *I* was fine."

"That's not an answer," she said stubbornly.

"Yes, Sharma, I'm alright."

Kiara let out a relieved shudder. "What's–" her voice broke. Krish reached out and squeezed her hand. "What's ... I ... *help*!"

Krish nodded. "Now listen carefully, okay? I need you to go home, see your dad, tell him you're okay. I told him we took a small overnight trip to Lonavala to cover up. Stick to that. Maybe take a shower? Read your mother's letter. Then wear oven mitts and open the locket. It's been two days since your birthday, but I promise, by the end of today, everything will be clear."

Kiara wanted to ask him about a million questions, but the pleading look in his eyes demolished her curiosity. She just nodded and wiped fresh tears off his cheeks.

"Hey, I'm fine. You don't need to worry, okay?"

He gave her a grim nod, pointed to the bathroom door and handed her her favourite pair of jeans, one of her shirts and clean undergarments. She awkwardly bundled the blanket around herself and limped across this strange place to the washroom.

While on her way, Kiara could've sworn she felt her wrists throb when she saw metal chains strung around the silver-grey pole in the middle of the room.

A few minutes later, she emerged, fully dressed, from the extremely unhygienic washroom. She made her way to the door but was startled to feel a hand on her shoulder.

"Hey," Aisha said, "thought you might need this."

She handed Kiara her purse and her mother's locket in a small pouch.

"Thanks. Aisha, I–where'd you come from?"

"I've just been ... around." A long, awkward pause ensued. "I wouldn't wear that," Aisha said finally, pointing at the pouch with the locket.

"What? Why not?" Kiara put her hand into the pouch to retrieve the locket, but screamed in pain and snatched it back as she felt her skin sizzle. She turned her fingers around to see a sizeable burn. When she turned to her friend, Aisha just shrugged sadly.

"You can't go home like that, Kiara."

"Now's really not the time to poke fun at my fashion sense, Aisha. Besides, what's wrong with my outfit?"

Aisha rolled her eyes. "I meant your shoulder."

Kiara winced as Aisha rubbed a serum into the wound and bandaged her up, slowly, gently.

"Thank you," she said as she put on the other girl's jacket to conceal the injury.

"Hey," Aisha said, her voice close to a whisper, "I know everything is confusing right now, and you're probably scared out of your mind. But I promise it's all going to work out. And, um, avoid anything silver."

Her palm grazed Kiara's cheek briefly, and then she was gone.

Kiara was many things in that moment: confused, angry, annoyed, hungry and, most of all, scared. She pulled her phone out of the purse, ignored the endless stream of texts from her father and almost sobbed as the familiar route home flickered across the screen.

Google Maps truly was mankind's greatest invention.

"There she is! Did you have fun?" Her dad sounded cheerful as he pulled her into a fatherly one-armed hug.

Kiara nodded and put on a smile, before pulling away gently. "Fun?" she echoed.

"Krish told me you guys took a small trip to Lonavala." Oh, right.

She smiled exaggeratedly and said, "Right, yes. It was great." Then, after a small pause, she added, "Papa, it's time." He nodded, and wordlessly walked her to his room. Kiara's heartbeat accelerated as he turned to her with a brown envelope that read, *Kiara: 18.*

"Thank you," she said, grasping it, then hurriedly walked out of his room, past the kitchen and into her bedroom.

Kiara ran fervent, trembling fingers across her mother's handwriting. It was a thick, heavy cursive. She clumsily tore open the envelope. A thick but small piece of paper landed on her lap. It read:

Dear Kiara,

If you are reading this letter, it means I am no longer with you. There are a million things I wish I could put down in here. How much I wish I could be with you and celebrate today, how beautiful and grown up I'm sure you are by now, how I'd love to get to know the young woman you've grown into. But most importantly: I'm sorry. I'm so, so sorry for leaving you and your father. I want you to know that I'm always watching over you.

With all my love,
Mumma

Kiara let the tears fall instead of blinking them away as she always did. She sat there, unmoving, reading the too-short letter over and over again. She licked her lips and tasted salt. A knock on the door brought her back to reality.

"Everything all right?"

Wiping her tears hurriedly, she let out a strangled, "Yes, Papa!" She didn't think he bought it, but was grateful that he let her be.

Only when wiping away her tears did she notice how horribly dirty she was. Stepping into the shower, she was pleasantly surprised to find a small scratch where a bloody wound had existed mere hours ago. She let the hot water soothe her and scrubbed herself four times over, stopping only when her skin turned red. No matter how many times she washed herself, she did not feel clean. Later, she tiptoed into the kitchen to retrieve some oven mitts. Slipping them on, she pulled out the locket and gently pried it open, no easy feat owing to the thick gloves. A small chit fell out of the locket.

Kiara recognized her mother's perfect handwriting at once. It said: *Come to the outskirts of Aarey Colony. Krish will be waiting for you.*

How had she known Krish? What was going on? Why Aarey Colony of all places, the forested area that was famously unsafe? Kiara grabbed her sneakers. Hating herself, she told her father she would be at Advik's.

She needed answers and she was going to get them. Now.

4

"I'M FINE. YOU don't need to worry, okay?"

Krish knew that Kiara had been trying to make him feel better, but somehow, he felt worse. *She* was the one comforting *him*, despite all the lies he'd told her.

He hadn't sobbed in years, but when he saw her lying unconscious like that, looking so broken and small, he wasn't able to hold back tears. Usually, only eighty per cent of them survived the transition. And given that Kiara was not normal, even in their world, the chances of her survival were slim. A little *too* slim. She meant more to Krish than he wanted to admit, and he couldn't imagine losing her.

The previous night came back to him in hazy flashes: Kiara's transformation, seven fully armed people running to his aid when he screamed for backup and finally, knocking Kiara out after numerous failed attempts and multiple injuries. He remembered gently laying the wolf down, making sure there was a pillow under her head and blankets around her massive form. He recalled using a thick towel to pry open Kiara's locket and slipping a small note in.

As much as he tried to shake the image out of his head, the only thing he saw when he closed his eyes were Kiara's helpless brown ones when she woke up, pleading for his help.

Pull yourself together, a voice in his head chided, *she needs you now more than ever.*

Krish was still in the basement. Kiara had left just a few minutes prior. Feeling the need to cleanse himself of this horrifying environment, he made his way out the door.

"Hey, wait up!" Advik called.

"Yeah?"

"You okay, man?"

"I'm fine!" It came out a lot louder and harsher than he had intended.

"Okay." Advik paused, then spoke gently, "And hey, Kiara's gonna make it, she's a fighter."

"Thanks."

Krish considered all his friends his family. But no one was more like a sibling to him than Kiara. A lump formed in his throat at Advik's words. He nodded at his friend, turned around and walked towards the forest to finally tell his best friend the truth he'd been keeping from her for more than a year.

Kiara was already there when he arrived. She seemed to have heard his footsteps and approached him.

Her tone was unbearably patient as she said, "How about those answers I was promised?"

Krish knew Kiara well enough to look through her outer calm at the curiosity that was eating her up inside. "Sharma, I need you to trust me, okay? Can you do that?"

"Of course," Kiara said with such sincerity that Krish's heart broke a little.

"Just follow me."

She nodded and put on a brave smile as he led her into the woods, exactly as he had been instructed.

Standing in the midst of the forest clearing was Anjali Sharma. Krish looked at Kiara to see how she would react. The colour had drained from her face. He was sure Kiara had seen pictures of her mother and would recognize her. Kiara looked at him, clearly expecting him to be as shocked as she was, but he had known about this for more than a year now.

Krish had expected a thousand different reactions from Kiara on seeing her 'resurrected' mother. But never in a million years would he have anticipated what happened next.

Fire danced in her eyes. It looked terrifyingly real, feral. Jaw hardening, she balled up her palm into a fist, then walked up to Krish and smacked him. He was sure he'd just imagined the shockingly high temperature of her fist as it collided with his face.

He was shocked, not because he was bleeding, but because Kiara had made him bleed. He'd never thought her weak, but he'd never imagined Kiara could use her strength against him.

An expression of hurt crossed her face, but it was overpowered by fierce, cold rage. Krish was ashamed of the thought that occurred to him: *she's acting like one of them.*

Kiara didn't even feel herself lose control. She was pleased to see blood trickling down Krish's nose.

"Sharma, wha–" he spluttered, looking flustered and disbelieving.

Then she really lost it. "Shut UP, Krish. Just shut up, you–"

She wasn't proud of this, but at that moment she reached into her mental dictionary, fished out the most vile, unprintable words she could think of and hurled them at him. Wrath—obstinate and undying—boiled inside her, taking over every cell in her body, till she was trembling with fury. She didn't care that her mother was watching, she didn't care that she was hurting her best friend. She just *didn't care.*

Kiara examined her hand and wiped Krish's blood on her clothes. Then, still shaking, she turned to face her mother, who just stood and stared at her, tears trickling down her face.

Anjali was short, curvy, slightly plump, wearing a simple, elegant black floor-length dress. She looked just like she did in the framed picture that Kiara's dad kept in his room. Her skin was the same olive as Kiara's, her eyes the same brown.

Anjali rushed towards her daughter and hugged her tight. A part of Kiara wanted to desperately hug her mother back and sob, but she was still unbelievably furious. She pulled away from Anjali harshly, wiping away tears of anger, and glared at the stranger in front of her.

"Really, Mumma? After the letter you wrote me, after leaving dad and me for more than a decade, you think you can just hug me and I'd be okay with everything? I've lived without a mother for almost as long as I can remember. Why show up now?"

Her mother winced almost unnoticeably. Kiara steadied her breathing as she turned on Krish.

"I came here for answers. You swore you would explain everything. Or was that just another one of your lies?" Kiara asked coldly.

He flinched and she felt proud. Whatever part of her still cared about his feelings was overruled by her desire to hurt him like he'd hurt her. Krish had seen all the times she had been on the verge of tears, wishing she had had a mother to talk to. He had always been calm and patient and had cheered her up somehow. He had said that everything would be okay. But in that moment, Kiara was unsure if anything he'd ever told her was true. How long had he known?

"Sharma, I just–"

"Don't you dare call me that! That was what my best friend called me, but I can't seem to find him."

He looked like she had just punched him again, but nodded and gestured towards her mother.

"Well ...?" she demanded, looking from Krish to her mother furiously. "What's happening to me?"

"Kiara, do you ever hear any weird animal sounds late at night?" her mother asked cautiously.

"Stray dogs," Kiara answered automatically.

"Think harder," Krish prompted gently.

"What do you mean, think harder, you–" Kiara began, but a thought struck her. "*Oh.* Wolves."

"Close enough. Think about what happened to you last night. What you felt, what you saw. Do you remember transforming?"

Kiara shuddered as the memories of the previous night rushed in. "How can any of that have been real? It felt like something out of a book, like I was a–"

Krish smiled slightly.

"What ... werewolf? How am I supposed to believe that?"

Her mother took over. "Werewolves have been around for centuries, and have surrounded you for much of your life. A human can get infected by a werewolf's scratch if they're under eighteen years of age. Once infected, the human 'Turns' but only when they become eighteen. A scratch received after the age of eighteen is as harmless as an ordinary dog bite. The person remains unaffected.

"I was fifteen when I got scratched. Your father and I were already together, and God, were we in love. The way teenagers are. On my eighteenth birthday, when I Turned, I was disgusted with myself.

"I didn't think it would be safe for me to live close to your father or my family. Luckily, I had a friend who was also a werewolf. Shweta Oberoi."

"Your–"

"My mother, yes," Krish confirmed.

"She knew about this portal in Mumbai that, even having lived here my whole life, I was unaware of."

"Portal?" Kiara started, but Krish shot her a familiar look that carried an unsaid message: *patience.*

"She suggested it would be best if we left our pasts behind and moved to Ordenia, painful as it was, for the wellbeing of our loved ones. So, we staged our deaths and fled." Anjali turned to look at Kiara again. "I made peace with not being able to be with your father because I knew I was doing the right thing by leaving. But he never believed I was dead, and hunted me down somehow. It took him years, but he did it. One day he just showed up here and said he would never ask about my past, that he just wanted to be with me regardless. I was young and weak–I broke down and agreed to let him stay here.

"Majority of Mumbai's population is werewolves, but there are some exceptions. Your friends Rishika and Hritik, for example. Your father. It was all right for them to stay here, until thirty years ago."

Kiara raised her eyebrows and scowled.

"Another thing about regular werewolves: after our eighteenth birthdays, we Turn every blue moon. But we're still us. We think straight, and are in complete control of our actions. Once we're back to our human state, we remember our Turning, every minute of it. Except the first time.

"Questions later, Kiara," she said as she saw her daughter opening her mouth to ask something. "There is also a different kind of werewolves, a very rare kind. They're called the Katrols. They completely lose their sense of self after their Turning. It's like a part of their soul temporarily leaves them. They cannot think straight, or differentiate friend from enemy. When they Turn, they become wild, untamed beasts with glowing red eyes, and kill everyone in sight. There have been no known Katrols for centuries. But now, there are two."

She hesitated. "The identity of the first one is still unknown," she said. "But the other," she continued with a shudder, "is you."

5

KRISH STARED AT Kiara as her jaw dropped and she digested the news. He watched as her body shook, and fought the urge to yell at Anjali for not being gentle enough with her. Tears flowed freely down her cheeks, and Krish could see her visibly struggling not to fully break down.

After a few moments, wiping her eyes, Kiara said quietly, "Well, isn't it obvious, then?"

Anjali and Krish exchanged confused glances.

Kiara took a deep breath. "You have to kill me. I'm too dangerous. I could hurt someone, I could–"

"NO!" The scream clawed its way out of Krish's throat.

"Mr Oberoi, please show Kiara to her room," was Anjali's only response.

Kiara wordlessly followed Krish, refusing to meet his gaze, hurt and rage still etched across her face. Miserably, Krish did as he was taught. He shut his eyes, letting himself get lost in the whisper of magic that emanated from the heart of the forest. Kiara gasped when she saw his normally black eyes lined with green. An identical greenish glow began to radiate from a tree a few metres to the left of where they were standing. He led her towards it, and pulled on a branch from the top. A wooden door automatically slid down. Ornate designs and gold lines wove their way through the door. Krish gestured to her to walk through first. She turned the doorknob with her shaking hands and couldn't conceal the gasp that escaped her lips as the door opened.

Before their eyes lay a scenic view: sleek towers of varied proportions grazed the sky, a gigantic glass building at the centre sparkled as sunlight kissed its surface and a large water body glittered in the distance. Grocery stores, gyms, restaurants and hotels were scattered around the market area. A long train snaked through their midst. This was a city in itself.

Krish led Kiara to a simple yet elegant white building. They walked up two flights of stairs in silence, until he slid a hand into his pocket and fished out a key to unlock a door.

"This is your room," he said.

A moderately sized, well-furnished, white room stared back at Kiara. Krish lingered awkwardly for a moment, before placing the key on a side-table in the room and reaching for the door, only to find Kiara's fingers wrapped around his wrist, tugging him back into the room.

"I need answers," was all she said.

"Right. Of–of course, ask me anything," he stammered, finally forcing himself to look into her face.

She looked pale and shaken. His heart contracted at the pain and exhaustion in her brown eyes.

"So, what–" she started. "What is this place?"

"It's called Ordenia. Portals to Ordenia are scattered across major cities all around the world, and in places with high werewolf populations. The newly Turned, like you–called the fledgelings–are found and brought here to adjust to their new life. They're trained in the ways of werewolf ... ery," he finished lamely.

An uncomfortable silence ensued, so he went on, "Two years of service to Ordenia is mandatory. After that, you can pursue life here, but there are some who want as little to do with werewolves as possible. They go back to the human world and come here only once a month, at full moon. There's a large thicket where we go to Turn every month."

"When you say 'trained', what do you mean?"

"We're trained in combat. If you choose to stay and work here, you'll need it. If you don't, it's just precautionary."

"Work here?"

"There are a few options for jobs here: you can track down fledgelings and mentor them, work to maintain Ordenia or hunt down the werewolves who go rogue and start killing and Turning innocents for the thrill of it. Training comprises combat classes, practical classes on our origins, history and magic. We're also taught labour–how to build basic things and use tools–to discipline and strengthen us."

"Huh." Kiara formulated her next question in prickly quietude. "Is there any kind of a werewolf governing body?"

"Yes, they're called the Alphas. It is a group of up to six werewolves, headed by a president. Our current president is Neil Raven."

Kiara nodded and cleared her throat. "About my-my kind ... have they ever been t-tamed?"

He looked at her to see her staring back at him curiously. "No," he answered feebly. "Usually, Katrols are hunted. But your mother met with the Alphas and convinced them to let us try to tame you, so we're going to give it our best. If we succeed, everything will be fine." He didn't tell her what would happen if they failed, and she didn't ask.

"Tell me about your time here," she said.

There wasn't much to be said there, but he told her everything he could. "I have no idea when I got scratched, or who did it. But I've been told it happened when I was ten. A lot of werewolves are scratched by their own family members, because they want them to be a part of this world. Or they're scratched by rogue werewolves who hunt for sport.

"Advik helped me through my whole ordeal, which was a rough job. He'd only been here about three weeks, but had adjusted quickly, as he'd been scratched by his own father at his own insistence. He slept in a room interconnected to mine, so he could rush to my side if I woke up from nightmares, sweating and screaming. He cleaned up my puke when I was overwhelmed and sick, and endured my unreasonable screaming at him. He was patient and kind and so inspiring that the day my training ended, I knew I wanted to help people the way he had helped me. So, when I turned nineteen, that's what I opted to do.

"The transition period is not easy, and I've been assigned to mentor you. In the period between the end of your training and your nineteenth birthday, you're assigned menial tasks, like working in the records room, or babysitting a werewolf's kid while their parents are on missions."

"What does my mother do?"

"She's the head of this sect of Ordenia."

"That night ... there was some kind of beeping before–before it happened, and you said, 'I was right'."

"Katrols' eyes glow red when they Turn. I saw it happen, and knew you were one, so I called for backup. Of course, your mother assigned you to me. She was with you when you were scratched, and knew this day would eventually come. I had an inkling that you were not a regular werewolf."

"How could you tell?"

"Katrols are ruled by their emotions. They're short-tempered and snap easily. The beast inside them needs an outlet–" He broke off mid-sentence and winced. "I ... I'm so sorry, Sharma– Kiara," he said, his voice breaking. "I'm sorry that a Katrol bit you. I'm sorry I hid so much from you. I'm sorry I didn't tell you about your mother. I'm sorry I–"

Kiara gestured at him to stop talking. "It's okay," she whispered. She squeezed his hand.

He looked at their intertwined fingers and a tentative smile pulled at the corner of his mouth.

"And don't ever call me Kiara again, I beg of you," she said.

He grinned at her. "Boy, do you know how to throw a punch."

She grinned back. "Why couldn't you just have told me about meeting me in Aarey? And how did you manage to prize open my locket?"

"I wanted to give you time and space to digest everything," he admitted. "And Anjali taught me how to open the locket. I had to whisper your name to it."

Kiara frowned at the mention of her mother, and gasped as a wave of epiphanies hit her. "You were talking to my mother on the phone on Friday. You haven't been travelling all summer. You mentioned that Advik trained you, he's one of us. I saw Aisha outside the basement, so she is too."

"Yes."

"And how were you ever allowed to attend classes if you graduated from school ... two years ago?"

"Wolf magic," he replied and watched her eyes widen. "I will tell you all about it, but I really think you should rest now, you've had quite a day."

"One last question for tonight–what has happened to others like me?"

"Katrols even existing is an extremely rare occurrence. We only know of two in our vicinity, because most Katrols today are undiscovered and just killed by humans under the impression that they're feral wild animals. And honestly, I want to tell you, we have answers about everything that has happened, is happening and will happen to you. I really do. But the truth is, you're the first Katrol we've managed to integrate into Ordenia. The rest are usually hunte–"

She flinched, and he opened his mouth to say something, perhaps *I'm sorry*, but she cut him off. "It's all right. Please take care of Dad, he'll be worried sick about me." He nodded and she smiled gratefully.

"You want me to stay next door for a bit?"

"Could you stay here?"

He smiled gently. "Of course. Scoot over."

She did. He kicked off his shoes, threw his jacket on the floor and got into bed beside her. There was nothing unusual about this; as far as they were concerned, Krish and Kiara were siblings.

Kiara yawned and buried herself under the blanket. "It was fun smacking you."

"Oh, just sleep already."

"'Night."

"Kie?" Krish said loudly as he shook her awake. She had been squirming and screaming for the last few minutes. She sat up with a start, and he saw tears streaming down her face. She grabbed his arm.

"Krish?" she said in a broken and quivering voice.

"Yes, it's me. You're okay; it's okay." He squeezed her shoulder. "Bad dream?" She nodded. "You feel like talking about it?"

"It was a full moon night," Kiara explained. "I was hanging out with you guys one minute, and the next, I was out of control. I was this wild thing, this–this animal with a thirst for blood. I felt that desire, Krish. I wanted to slice everyone's throats open, and drink their blood and–and tear off chunks of your flesh to savour. I–I woke up in a pool of blood and then I saw ... I saw–" She broke off as fresh tears poured down her face. "I saw bodies, Krish. Yours, Mom's, Dad's, Rish's and Advik's. I won't–I can't become that murderer. I need you to promise me that if things get out of hand, you'll kill me. If you were ever my best friend, if you ever cared about me, please just do it. *Promise me!*"

He thought about it. A huge part of him wanted to scream that he could never do that to her, and that it was ridiculous of her to even *ask* such a thing of him.

But the other part saw her side. She had just been told that she would transform into a sadistic, murderous monster once a month. He knew that had he been in her shoes, he, too, would have wanted assurance that he wouldn't be allowed to hurt the ones he loved. So, he made his decision with a heavy heart, hoping it would never come to that. "I promise. I won't let anything happen."

She wiped the tears off her cheeks. "You sleepy?" she asked him.

He didn't think he could go back to sleep, so he shook his head. "I guess not. Why?"

"I'm tired of this. I'm tired of this fear and helplessness. I want to fight. Can you teach me?" She frowned.

"It's four o'clock in the morning, Kie."

"And?"

"And ... I can teach you." She smiled a little. "I'm going to freshen up, and I guess you could, too. Some of your clothes are in that wardrobe," he said, pointing at the single white cupboard in the corner of the room.

"How did you–"

"Don't ask."

"Well, thanks. And Krish?"

"Yeah?"

"I'm sorry I punched you."

"Go change, Kie," he said, hiding a smile.

6

"WHERE ARE WE off to?" Kiara asked. "The training room. You didn't happen to spot that enormous glass tower, did you?" Krish grinned.

Kiara's jaw dropped. "No way in *hell* is such a beautiful building a place for training."

Krish shrugged, a knowing gleam in his eyes.

"What?" Kiara demanded. "What?"

He just winked at her. "Follow me."

She cursed, but fell into step beside him. He had the audacity to chuckle. She glared daggers at him, he stared back and winked again. She groaned and elbowed him.

"Hey, cut it out!" he whined.

She rolled her eyes at him, and was about to make a snarky comeback when–

"We're here."

Kiara had thought the tower looked stunning in daylight. In the dark, it looked nothing short of magical. Moonlight bounced off its crystalline surface. The interiors were lit up by gorgeous blue lights and gave the illusion of raining crystals.

Krish smiled at the wondrous look on her face as he escorted her up two flights of stairs. She clamped her gaping mouth shut, a little embarrassed, and composed herself enough to bombard him with the questions she hadn't asked the night before.

"What am I going to learn here?"

"I'm going to have you try out as many weapons as needed, until you find something you like, something you identify with. Something that feels like a part of you that's been missing your whole life; something that completes you."

"Are you talking about some weapon, or a certain someone?" Kiara was surprised to see him turn away quickly, as if concealing something from her. "What is happening?"

Krish changed the subject quickly. "This is it," he said.

Kiara was getting seriously annoyed with how perfect this place was. She stared at a classy, cream-coloured room. Bows, arrows, daggers, knives, longswords, throwing stars, guns and other arms adorned the walls. The floor was lined with a plush mattress to cushion falls. Her eyes landed on the huge glass window, and lit up as she took in the view: the entirety of Ordenia could be seen asleep now, the dark buildings only barely visible in the moonlight.

"This place is ..." Kiara started. "I mean, it's just ..."

Krish only said, "I know."

She took a few moments to take everything in, and was grateful Krish knew her well enough to give her space. He just hung back and pretended to examine a set of golden arrows.

Finally, she took a deep breath. "Tour time's over. Teach me."

Krish carefully set the arrows back on their stands. His gaze met hers. *You okay?* he seemed to ask. She nodded.

He assessed her face and said, "This part could take a while, okay? You just have to go through the room, try out the weapons and see what calls your name. There's no hurry."

He sounded confident. Kiara nodded, then proceeded to slowly skim through the weapons, trying her hand at almost all of them. She tried shooting with the golden arrows, then firmly decided arrows were really not her thing, after having almost impaled Krish the third time in a row. The arrows weren't the only things she'd hurt him with. She kept accidentally hitting him to the point where he felt the need to ask, "Are you still mad at me, Sharma? If that's the case, I'd really rather you throw another punch at me."

He then proceeded to dodge faux bullets and gave a weak smile when she apologized, but cautiously and quickly prized the gun out of her hands. Eventually, he gave her a tired look that could only mean, *Let's call it a night.*

Kiara withheld a scream when something suddenly tugged at her. She couldn't resist the pull. Her feet moved against her will, and planted themselves so she faced the walls that held the daggers. Her hands went to a dainty silver one that was curved at the edges and had a beautiful ash grey hilt. As soon as she touched it, it felt *right* in her hands. Kiara felt energy coursing through her veins. She felt truly alive. She turned to face Krish, and he nodded approvingly.

"This isn't just a weapon, you need to understand that. It becomes a true companion, and it recognizes the familiar touch of its master. It becomes a part of you, and losing it is pretty rare and painful, like losing a friend. There's even a bonding ceremony that happens once you turn nineteen, for you and your weapon. That gives you enough time to get acquainted with it, and to really see it as more than a material object. It needs to feel perfect in your hands."

Kiara nodded. That sounded about right.

"And, um, I know this might sound stupid, but you've got to name the blade."

"Like what?"

"People name their weapons after anything from flowers to their parents, but I want something original." His eyes challenged her.

She nodded and closed her eyes, racking her brain, trying to think of a name. When she opened them again, she had an answer.

"This blade marks a new beginning for me," she said. "So I'll call it Dawn."

Krish raised his eyebrows in slight surprise. "Okay, Kie. Let's see how good you are at this. And be careful with that. That silver is going to *hurt* if it touches me."

"Well, I'm just a beginner ... shouldn't you make me use wooden sticks or something?"

"I should," he agreed, making no move to pry the dagger from her. "Well then, I should probably teach you some basics."

He proceeded to show her numerous methods of thrusting, slashing and catapulting using Dawn. She replicated them, some manoeuvres taking longer to learn than others.

"That should be good enough for our first trial round," Krish said approvingly. "In the centre of the room, if you will."

They circled one another. Krish lunged, his long sword aiming for her face. She dodged the blade and aimed Dawn at his stomach. He deflected easily. They parried for a few moments, the metal clinking deafeningly. As he focused his strength on pushing his sword against Dawn, she executed a sideways kick at his arm. His sword landed softly on the cushioned floor. Krish looked shocked, impressed and ... upset? Happy? Angry?

"S-sorry," she murmured.

"Sorry?" he repeated, incredulous. "That was brilliant, Sharma. Where did you learn how to do that?" His face broke into his classic goofy grin.

"I don't know. Instinct?"

"All right. What else you got?"

She felt the corner of her lips tugging into a small smile, and swung her dagger at him, yelling delightedly as they engaged in combat.

Half an hour later, they were both panting, dripping with sweat, but smiling. As it turned out, Kiara was a born fighter.

"How was that, *coach*?" she said smugly, offering a hand to pull Krish up from the floor.

"Don't get ahead of yourself. Seriously, though, how *did* you do that?"

Kiara just beamed.

"How about we take a breather from the lessons? You go freshen up and meet me in my room once you're done. There are some people I want to introduce to you."

She raised her eyebrows, but agreed. She offered Dawn back to Krish, not really knowing what to do with it, but he shook his head. "You have to keep that," he said, ruffling through the drawers on a wall. "Here." He handed her a leather cover for the blade.

"What's this for?" she said, pointing at the hook attached to the back of the sheath.

"You'll get a weapon belt soon."

"All right, then," she said, sheathing Dawn. "I'll see you in a bit."

Kiara walked out of the room, feeling more like herself than ever before.

A little while later, as Krish had instructed, Kiara knocked on his door. “Hey, it’s me.”

She heard Krish speaking to someone in a hushed voice. He opened the door to let her in and gestured to his bed. There were two people sitting there—a girl and a boy. The girl was shockingly pretty and appeared to be slightly shorter than Kiara. Her long, straight black hair looked striking against her chocolate brown skin. Next to her sat the most gorgeous person Kiara had ever seen. She had to bite her lip to keep from gasping, because how embarrassing would *that* be?

He looked around Krish’s age. He was lean, but his muscles were prominent under a white sweatshirt, and even though he was sitting, she could tell he was very tall. He had the most striking turquoise eyes, short, curly black hair, sharp, angular cheekbones and a small scar near his left eyebrow. He was smiling slightly. Kiara felt her heart flutter as she smiled back at him.

“Um,” Krish began, obviously uncomfortable.

Kiara extended her arm and squeezed his shoulder reassuringly. Was it just her or did two pairs of eyes keenly follow the trail of her arm?

Krish smiled gratefully. “You know how you’ve been asking me for the last few years why I’m not interested in any of the girls at school?” he said.

“Where is this going?”

“I—uh, I have a girlfriend, actually.” Krish blushed nervously and beckoned the girl forward. She walked to him and laced her fingers with his. He seemed to like it, as his cheeks grew redder still.

Kiara felt her face fall. Krish had been her best friend for as long as she could remember, and they had never kept any secrets from each other. Everything from their deepest fears to how many rotis they'd had for lunch, they shared. Keeping the werewolf world from her was one thing; it was for her safety. But this? This had to do with his personal life. Kiara felt yet another secret chip away at her unwavering trust in her childhood best friend.

"Kiara, this is Amara Paige. She's from the States. Amara, Kiara Sharma."

"Hi," Amara said in a beautiful, silky voice.

Kiara thought she saw a flash of distaste (and fear?) flickering in Amara's eyes, which went as suddenly as it came, and left her thinking she had imagined it.

"Hi," Kiara replied, grinning. If the other girl thought Kiara was strange, at least she was polite enough not to show it.

"She's the most intelligent person I've ever met," Krish said proudly.

"Krish!" Amara chided in mock modesty, but Kiara could see that she was grinning.

"And this," Krish said, pointing at the boy, *finally*, "is Aidan."

Did Krish know he was talking about a *god*?

"Holy handsome," Kiara breathed as he extended a hand.

"Sorry?" he said.

Her eyes widened, mortified she had said that out loud. "H-hey, Aidan," she said. She liked her voice when she said his name.

He gave her a stunning smile. "Hey."

She felt ... jittery?

"Aidan is our good friend. He specializes in weapons," Amara told her.

"You should train with her, Aidan," Krish added, pointing at Kiara. "It was her first session today, and she was damn near better than me."

Kiara felt her cheeks redden as Aidan gave her an impressed glance, while Amara frowned slightly. Kiara figured it was because Krish really was an amazing fighter, or maybe she didn't like anyone beating her boyfriend.

"All right, Kiara. Tomorrow at 1:00 p.m. You and me. Training room."

"You're on," replied Kiara, surprised at how steady her voice was. "And call me Kie."

Krish raised his eyebrows; it had taken him a full three weeks to earn back his 'Kie' rights.

"You too," Kiara said to Amara as an afterthought.

"Can I talk to you for a second, Sharma?" Krish said.

"Sure."

They stepped out, and Krish shut the door behind him. It still alarmed Kiara how soundlessly Krish could move. He had crossed the room, opened and closed a door, all with almost zero noise.

"What?" she asked him, puzzled.

"You like him," he said simply.

"What?" she repeated, thrown off guard.

"Do you not like her?" he asked quietly.

"What are you talking about?"

"I just got the feeling something was ... off between you and Amara."

"What, in the three seconds we were in the same room?" He shrugged. "Krish, she seems great."

Relief broke out over his face, plain and unabashed. "Sorry, I guess I'm being paranoid. It's just–I really want you guys to get along."

"Hey, she seems amazing. I'm sure Amara and I will get along famously."

"She's one of *them*, Aidan." Amara sounded as incredulous as she felt. Had Ordenia learnt *nothing*?

"She has that aura which they have, I–" She broke off and shuddered. After Laura, after the pain she and many others of Ordenia experienced every day as a result of Kiara's kind, she couldn't believe the Alphas would be so stupid. Was it really that hard to understand? They couldn't be controlled, couldn't be tamed. Each was just as horrible and evil as the last. They needed to be put down, killed. She didn't understand why Ordenians wouldn't just hunt them down and do everyone a favour by ending their existence.

"Oh, Kiara seems perfectly lovely, of course, for a monster."

"This again, Mary? Not a day goes by that I don't think of Laura. Not a day goes by when I don't want to hunt down the people who took her life. What wouldn't I do to kill the one responsible. Or better yet, to have her back ..." Amara's eyes stung. "But we can't, can we? We can't have her back, she's gone." He put his hands on her shoulders. "I promise, we will get our revenge. But, I mean, did you see Krish the other day? Did you see how broken he was when he thought she wouldn't make it?"

Amara nodded. Of course, she'd seen him. She'd seen his normally perfect hair dishevelled, his eyes red and puffy. She'd heard his ragged sobs–as if he'd lost a piece of himself. She'd felt his tears on her shoulder as she'd held him. She'd seen the immeasurable joy on his face when Kiara had stirred. Amara had watched him talk to her from afar—and it looked like the other girl felt the same deep love for him.

Kiara had woken up from a horrible ordeal, but refused to see anything but the tears on Krish's face, hear the tremor in his voice. She'd heard Kiara's concerned questions, her murmured reassurances. She'd watched her wipe the tears from Krish's face. Something about the duo just ... clicked. Even a stranger could tell by the way they looked at each other, talked about one another, behaved in each other's presence that they shared a bond that ran deeper than blood.

As she thought this, Amara heard Laura's voice in her head: her flowery laugh, her bold accent, her tough but oddly consoling words. Laura was, and had always been, Amara's angel. Her light in the dark. A light that had been extinguished by a Katrol.

"... have to at least try," Aidan was saying. "Amara? Are you even listening to me?"

"Yeah, that's true," Amara said distractedly.

Aidan's brows furrowed in confusion. He rolled his turquoise eyes and let out a defeated sigh. "Point is," he said, patting Amara on the back, "we have to give her a fair chance. They're not all the same. So just try to let it go, for Krish."

"For Krish," she echoed. "I'll let it go."

But she knew she wouldn't let it go. Though it wasn't her fault, Kiara was a monster. A monster living in Amara's home, hiding in plain sight.

And she'd be damned if she didn't do anything about it.

7

HE WAS POLISHING a gorgeous set of green-hilted daggers. Kiara was about to knock on the door to the training centre when she noticed Aidan, his face a painting of concentration—eyes focused, brows furrowed, lips still. She let her hand drop from the door handle and watched the graceful movements of his body. His left palm gently cradled the daggers, his right carefully cleaning them. She stared, transfixed, at the synchronicity of his muscled arms, at his dark curls falling over his forehead.

She forced her eyes away from him to the wall of weapons a few inches to his left.

"Hey," said a voice from behind her. Instantly, Kiara had grabbed the intruder's arm and was ready to twist it when—

"Whoa," said Aidan, a smile lighting up his features. "I would love to see what happens next, but I'm afraid I like my bones to stay in their sockets."

Kiara cursed herself and opened her mouth to mumble an apology, when Aidan cut in, "Don't. I'm okay, and that was pretty cool."

"Thanks," Kiara said.

"And I do apologize for scaring you." Aidan smirked. He caught sight of the sheath in her hand. "Let's see it. Weapon geek, remember?"

She unsheathed Dawn and handed it to him carefully. Kiara felt the calluses and rough edges on his hands as they brushed hers. His eyes widened as he saw Dawn. He ran his fingers over the curves of the dagger, not even flinching as the silver made contact with his skin.

"Hey!" Kiara said, snatching his hand away from the dagger. There was a fresh wound on his palm.

"I'm alright. I'm used to it, really." He sounded amused.

Kiara flushed, embarrassed.

"This dagger has been in this place for seventy-two years now. The next oldest one is about four and a half years old," he said, an excited glint in his eyes.

She was still confused. "Okay, and that means ...?"

"This blade has not appealed to anyone in more than seven decades," he said. He looked straight into her eyes. "You're special, Kiara Sharma."

"Thanks," she said, blushing furiously, and hurried to distract him. "Should we get down to business?"

His lips tugged upwards in response. Aidan grabbed two identical bronze daggers from his belt and handed Dawn back to Kiara. Both of them took their preferred fighting stances.

"Ready?" he asked.

"Ready."

Kiara sliced Dawn through the air in an arc. One of Aidan's daggers collided with it. Kiara grunted as she pressed the dagger downward with all her might, and gasped as Aidan jabbed the hilt of his other dagger into her stomach, enough to catch her off guard, but not enough to injure her. He used her momentary distraction to hook his foot around her leg, making her fall onto the cushioned floor. She aimed Dawn at his foot, but his dagger was there to meet hers. He plucked Dawn from her hand, threw the three blades to the side and pinned her to the floor. She wriggled vigorously, but his grip didn't loosen.

"Can't. Breathe," she gasped.

"You surrender?"

"No," she managed weakly. "I don't."

She rammed her shoulder into his. She had hoped that would distract him, but he appeared to have been anticipating it, as his grip grew tighter. Kiara still didn't budge. Aidan chuckled.

"Will you only surrender once I've actually killed you?"

"Not even then," she replied obstinately.

He stared at her. His lips slowly, almost reluctantly, curved upwards. Kiara was suddenly very aware of their closeness–his arms wrapped around her, his skin warm on hers, his eyes boring into hers, as if seeing through her. Aidan, as if also coming to the same realization, looked away hurriedly. The amusement in his eyes was replaced with intensity as he shook his head. When he looked back at her, that expression of–yearning?–was gone.

He cleared his throat. "Well, I'm personally not comfortable killing you. So, not because *you* have given up in any way, but because *I* have, I'm going to let you go. Is that all right?"

She nodded reluctantly. He moved his arms away from her waist after lingering for a moment.

"Krish *is* one of our best fighters ..." he said.

"But not better than you, I suppose?" she finished.

He grinned. "Your words, not mine."

He held out his hand to help her up, and she took it.

Hours flew by.

Kiara soon got a hang of Aidan's fighting style. He was heavily dependent on his right arm, and often kept his left side unguarded. She ducked a swing from his dagger and executed a sideways kick to his left shoulder. A satisfying wince reached her ears. He lunged for her arm, but she dodged swiftly.

Suddenly, the doors flew open. Advik emerged, looking ruffled. "There you are!" he called out to them. "Krish said you guys have been in here for the last two hours. What's going on?"

Aidan looked at her. "It can't have been that long."

She shrugged. Aisha walked in behind Advik, scowling. "You guys missed lunch!"

Advik shot her an incredulous look. "Oh, come on. Give her a break." He turned to Kiara. "So, how are you adjusting?"

Three pairs of curious eyes watched her. "Better than I thought I would," Kiara replied.

Aisha's gaze landed on her dagger-wielding arm. She looked at Aidan, then back at Kiara's hand. "Is that ...?" He nodded.

"How do you know about Dawn?" Kiara asked.

"Aidan never shuts up about it," Advik said. "Cool name, though."

Aidan's protest was lost in the flurry of their voices.

The group headed to the cafeteria, where Amara joined them. They were in the middle of tea a while later when Krish burst in, his face as white as a ghost.

Amara was the first to notice Krish. "What's wrong?"

"There's been an attack on Ordenia. Drop everything and tell everyone to get ready to fight."

8

KRISH SAW A wide range of reactions from the group around the table. Advik frowned at his half-eaten burger, and continued to look at his meal longingly while fidgeting around for his weapons. Aisha searched for her gun. Aidan pulled out his daggers, surprisingly calm. Amara looked like she was biting down hard on her tongue to keep herself from exploding with questions.

Krish turned to his best friend. The colour had drained from her face. Her eyes welled up as her lip trembled. He saw her struggle to keep from falling apart. Her quivering arm reached for Dawn. Fear and determination waged a war in her eyes.

"What? An attack? Is that common? Who's attacking us? What do we do? We fight, right? I'm *going* to fight. Am I–"

"Kie, *stop*." Krish tried to calm his racing heart. He turned to Advik and Aisha. "Guys, I need you to alert everyone. Make sure they're all armed and quickly assemble outside." The two sprinted away. "Aidan, Amara, report to Anjali. She wants to see you." Aidan nodded and took off. Amara dropped a light kiss on Krish's cheek before following him.

He turned to face Kiara. "And that leaves you, Sharma. Since you are newly Turned, you have the option to sit this one out." As soon as he said it, he realized his mistake. When given the option, Kiara would never choose to appear weak. He should have told her she wasn't allowed to participate, that she was ordered to stay out of it.

Kiara wiped her damp cheeks. Her grip on her dagger tightened. "Absolutely not," she choked out.

It was the answer Krish had been expecting from her. "Come on." He walked in quick strides, not sure where he was going.

"Krish, I was wondering, how long does my training last?"

"Two to three weeks, but it's at least a month before you get clearance to start preparing for your first real assignment. The preparation and special training can take anywhere from nine months to about three years, depending on the nature of the project."

"I was your first assignment, wasn't I?" Kiara asked.

Krish knew she was genuinely curious to hear his answer, but he couldn't tell her. Not yet. "You were the second. Don't ask, please. We're here, by the way."

Kiara looked confused.

It was an empty, box-like room, with seemingly misplaced shelves sticking out from every angle. The large set of windows on the ceiling made it look even odder.

"What do I do in here?" she asked.

"Nothing." Krish raced out of the room and bolted the door shut. "Sorry it had to be this way, Kie. You have to stay out of this one. Your safety is my responsibility."

Livid, Kiara pounded on the door and screamed obscenities at him. She begged him to come back and let her out. Krish didn't feel guilty as he walked away.

The battlefield was a chaotic bloodbath. The usually fresh grass was splattered with red. The air stank of blood and bullets. Krish's eyes scanned his surroundings for Advik and Aisha; they were nowhere to be seen. He spotted Amara hiding in the bushes, her arrow aimed at the blonde Aidan was sparring with.

Before he could analyze any further, Krish heard a gunshot behind him. He sprang aside just in time–the bullet barely grazed his ear. He turned around to see the attacker, but there was no one there. From another direction, a short, armed man made his way purposefully towards him. Krish yelled in frustration, raised his sword and raced into the heart of the battle.

This was the second time in two days that Kiara had wanted to murder her best friend.

She winced. A hole burned through her palm. She screamed in frustration and punched the wall. Tears of pain and rage clouded her vision. How could he just leave her locked in a room, with no way out? But there must be a way out. Then it hit her–the windowed ceiling! She forced open one of the cupboards, which, apart from the family of rats inhabiting it, was empty. Another was locked. The third one had nails poking out from the inside. She hopelessly pried open the fourth and was pleased to see the treasure it held.

Magnets, nails, an alarmingly large hammer and a few, very dusty blocks of wood. *Not a bad haul*, she thought.

Kiara grabbed a block of wood and threw it at the ceiling with all her might. She heard a satisfying crack, and sidestepped just in time to avoid the shards.

She brought out the rest of her supplies. Metal, wood, magnets, nails ... Kiara was creative. She got to work.

Aidan had almost died around four times already. He was now fighting a stunning blonde. The blonde suddenly shot him a dazzling smile and took advantage of Aidan's momentary distraction to stab him in the gut. Or he would have, had Aidan not sidestepped gracefully, a laugh bubbling out of him.

The man gave Aidan a flirty wink. "Hey there, gorgeous." Aidan spared him no thought as he drove one of his daggers into the blonde's stomach. He leant in and whispered, "Sorry it had to be this way, gorgeous," and let the blonde fall gracelessly to the ground.

Since Laura, Aidan had convinced himself that romance was nothing but a distraction. He had felt an unjustifiable amount of heartbreak at her death, even though their job had always been risky, with a constant threat of death looming over them at all times. Even though they'd only been going out for a few weeks. Even though he'd never told her he loved her. All feelings were a distraction, every single one–

He turned to see a familiar figure racing towards the battlefield. How could Krish have let her fight? Kiara looked victorious as she plummeted down the slope, Dawn glinting in her hand. Aidan stared in horror as she stabbed a young boy in the leg, and did not notice a scrawny girl running towards him, sword in hand.

He heard Krish yell, "Aidan!" and swerved out of the girl's way just in time, her sword barely missing his arm. He quickly disarmed the girl and had her panting on the ground in no time. She looked at him, her gaze full of searing hatred. Knowing he might regret it later, he slung the girl's sword around his hips and ran away from her, missing the surprised look on her face as he wove through the battlefield, towards Kiara.

"Three casualties, multiple injured," said Anjali Sharma, mere minutes after the enemy had retreated. "I have spoken with the Alphas and senior officers, and they wanted me to brief you all on a few things."

Krish, Kiara, Amara and Aidan were standing in Kiara's mother's office: a beige room with black accents, simple brown furniture and gleams of gold here and there.

"Still no sign of Advik or Aisha," Anjali said. Krish felt an ounce of guilt in his stomach. He hadn't thought about either of them in the chaos that had ensued. "We still don't know who led the attack," Anjali continued. "Kiara, you would do well to wait outside for a moment." Her eyes flashed dangerously. She also dismissed Amara, who had to be taken care of–a huge gash across her left foot that wouldn't stop bleeding. Krish's eyes followed her as she limped out of the room. After a minute of silence, Aidan cleared his throat.

Anjali continued, "Clearly, our warriors were thoroughly underprepared for this attack. We don't know if this ambush was just a one-time event, or if it will lead to a string of attacks. We have been so focused on our jobs that the fighters' preparedness for battle has been compromised. Henceforth, we need to double their training and conduct frequent drills. We also need new strategies in case something like this were to happen again. We need some people to do research on the enemy's identity and whereabouts. I can give you–"

At that moment, Advik and Aisha burst into the room. Krish took in their appearances. Advik's hair was dishevelled. There was a bloody gash across his forehead. Aisha's glasses were broken, blood trickling down from her nose. Kiara followed them in.

"What the hell happened?" Kiara asked.

"When the attack happened, we ran to the headquarters to get ourselves armed before going out. I took my weapons and turned around to find Aisha gone. I started to call her name, but someone came in from behind and knocked me out," Advik said.

Aisha continued, "Someone gave me this," she pointed to her bloody nose, "and shut me in the broom closet. It took a little longer than anticipated to break out of there. Once out, I saw Advik lying unconscious, and managed to wake him up. And then, we ran."

"What does all this mean?" Advik asked.

"I think the only thing it can mean," Krish said, "is that we have a spy in our midst."

9

"WHAT," ANJALI SAID, her voice dangerously calm, eyes blazing with fury, "were you thinking, going out there?" A few moments of awkward silence followed this question. Kiara's friends were still in the room, none of them knowing what to do after the bomb that had just been dropped on them. Advik, Aisha, Aidan and Krish dismissed themselves, their faces bearing identical expressions of confusion mixed with horror. When Krish nodded at Kiara curtly, a fresh bead of sweat trickled down her face. She knew she was in for a lecture from him, and though there was no one who she was closer to in the world, she also knew how scary his protective anger was.

Kiara now stood in her mother's office all alone, wishing she could be anywhere else. "Mumma, I had to do something," Kiara said, pleading Anjali to understand. "Krish and Aidan both admitted I'm a good fighter, and I couldn't have just stayed locked in there."

"So you break out and fight with one day of training? This is the result of the way your father raised you! Never to think, just do whatever comes to mind. So reckless, Kiara. So reckless! You saw your friends' faces when they saw you walk out there, didn't you? What would've happened to them had you been killed? And let me tell you, you could very well have! I just got you back after forever. It would have destroyed me to lose you again. You know that, right? So next time, *think*. You're a sharp child. You have a goddamned brain. You would do well to use it."

Kiara looked at Anjali as if she had just slapped her. She knew her mother was right, but fury bubbled up inside her, drowning out logic. "Yeah? Well, whose fault is it that Papa had to raise me, huh?" Kiara was surprised at how cold her tone was. "Whose fault is it that I was left in his care all my life? You can act as righteous as you want, Mumma, but you're not innocent either." She winced as a small spark snaked its way across her body.

Anjali looked appalled. "You should go," was all she said.

"No," Kiara said stubbornly. "I deserve to know what happened."

Anjali considered. "I suppose." She looked tired and weary, but Kiara just wanted answers. "Fire away."

"I want to know about the day it happened," Kiara said simply, and Anjali understood.

"You were just two years old. Your father and I had decided to move out of Mumbai as soon as possible after your birth because I had told him that a serial killer was after me, but really, I just didn't want you to become a werewolf. That is also the reason your father later believed that I was dead–because I had told him about a supposed serial killer." Kiara looked sceptical. "Oh, believe me," Anjali said in answer, "it was a very well-woven story. Even your father couldn't see the gaps in the thread."

This did explain to a large extent why Kiara's father had never questioned the car crash story, or the coincidence of the existence of the letters.

"Anyway, the only way one can become a Katrol is if one is scratched by a Katrol, and there was only one at the time, so I thought the odds of you being scratched by it were low. One afternoon, we were in the kitchen. Your father had gone to visit your grandmother, who was sick. I was feeding you when it happened. A Katrol broke in through our window and tore into the house. I fought it off, but it had already scratched you. I knew it had smelt the werewolf in me and had come to attack my family, though I don't know *why*. I'm so sorry, Kiara. I should have left Mumbai behind a long time ago. Then none of this would've happened, you wouldn't have Turned and I would still be with your father. I was, and still am, too attached to the city to let go, and that caused you to get scratched by that monster. But I had to get away from you before it could hurt you further. I knew you would Turn one day, and I would meet you then. But you couldn't know that I was alive a second sooner than you did. I made two copies of the letter I gave your father, because I knew I would have to explain everything to you one day. Here," she said, passing a piece of paper to her.

Kiara recognized that perfect handwriting instantly.

Dear Manohar,

By the time you read this letter, I will have died in what I'm assuming will be labelled as another 'car crash'. I'm going to tell you that it's probably not a car crash, but I am dead. He has probably got to me by now. I know you will want to search for me, but I'm not coming back this time. And our daughter's life is in your hands. I urge you to think of her, of little Kiara, first. I know it will be a difficult, exhausting and tumultuous journey, but you're a natural at being a father, and always have been. I have no doubt Kiara will turn out to be an incredible person. I'm sorry I had to leave you again. Just know that I love you.

Kiara said nothing.

"Kiara, I–I'm sorry that I left you all those years ago, but I did it to protect you. Sometimes you have to break someone's heart for their own good."

"Thanks, Mumma."

It was all Kiara could manage as she walked out of the room, her throat feeling like she'd swallowed a gallon of acid.

"Kiara?" Aidan said.

He knocked on her door for the fourth time. Just as he was about to give up and retreat, she appeared in the corridor. She was pale and sweaty, and there were dried bloodstains on her clothes and skin. Her gaze landed on him.

"Aidan?" she said, confused.

"Hey, I just wanted to check if you're okay," he said, then realized how stupid he sounded. It had been her first time actually fighting, actually killing. Of course, she wasn't okay. The sight of her trembling with what he supposed was sorrow, exhaustion and shock made him nervous in a way he hadn't been in a long time. But Kiara had Krish; she had Advik and Aisha. He'd known her for less than three days. Surely if she had a problem, she would consult one of her friends? So what was *he* doing here?

"Oh," Kiara replied weakly. "Come on in, then," she said, unlocking the door to her room.

Feeling awkward, Aidan made his way to the sofa in her room and watched her weary, mechanical movements as she picked out clothes from a closet.

"So how are you?" he asked finally.

She turned towards him, looking hopelessly lost. "What was I thinking?" she whispered, seemingly more to herself than to him. "Why did I go out there today? Krish was right, I shouldn't have gone. He was right to lock me up. I guess I was scared for my friends and wanted to do something for them." She sank onto the bed, not caring about her dirty clothes. She put her head in her hands and murmured through her fingers, "I had this–this need to be out there today, to fight. I craved it. I wanted to partake in the violence. I wanted to kill people. I had two people at sword-point. I was going to kill them, but I–I couldn't. I couldn't bring myself to push the blade in. To—" She cut off suddenly and ran to the bathroom, her hand over her mouth.

Aidan bolted in after her in alarm and saw her barely make it to the toilet before hurling her guts out. He was there in an instant, kneeling beside her, holding back her hair as she heaved, his hand making soothing circles on her back.

"Aidan, please–I don't w–want you to s–see me like this," she managed.

"Don't be ridiculous," he snapped.

She smiled weakly and almost finished saying 'thank you' before more bile rose up her throat. "So much for first impressions," she said.

"Hey," he said. "Don't worry about that, okay? Let's get you cleaned up." He supported her as she got up, and walked her to the bed. He hurried back to the bathroom and dampened a towel. He carefully wiped her face with it, tracing every plane and angle, every edge, every bit of the softness of her cheeks.

"You think you can manage a shower?" he asked. "I can ask Aisha to help you if–"

She cut him off with a vigorous shake of her head. "I can take a bath," she said, her voice trembling. He helped her back to the bathroom.

"I–I can go now if you want."

"Okay," she said.

But for some reason, he stayed.

When he heard the soft pitter-patter of the shower water hitting the floor, he finally let his tense muscles relax. He knew he should be thinking about his own self, how he was doing after the battle, but all he could see were Kiara's helpless eyes, her shaking body, the tears running down her beautiful face.

"Aidan?" she called from inside the bathroom. "Are you still there?"

"I'm here."

He didn't think he imagined the relief on her face as she came out.

"I can't button up my shirt, my hands are–" She raised her quivering hands.

"Come here," he said gently. He crossed the room, closing the space between them. His eyes met Kiara's large brown ones. He let out an exhale as he reached for her shirt and was surprised to find his own hands shaking slightly as he looped one button shut, then another. His fingers grazed her bare skin as he worked, sending shivers down her spine. His hands lingered at her waist as he finished with the last button. She looked up at him questioningly, and he flushed, letting his arms fall to the side. Her intense gaze didn't leave him. He scanned her face, her pink cheeks, her smooth jawline, her full lips ...

But then an image flashed through his mind: Laura's thin lips on his, her passionate touch, her whispered words. Her loud laugh, her fearless demeanour, her reckless mind. He shook his head, and Kiara's eyes bored into his. Then she looked away.

"Thank you," she said. "I don't usually let people see me like that."

"Don't mention it," he said, turning to move away. "Feel better soon."

But then her delicate fingers caught his wrist, sending a spark up his arm. "Could you not tell anyone about this?" she said, her eyes pleading. "I just don't want them to worry about me."

"But Kie–" he began, the nickname sliding off his tongue.

"Please, Aidan? Look, I'm fine."

"As long as you promise to ask for help if you need it."

"Okay," she said after a moment's hesitation. "I promise."

He nodded and noticed that her hand was still clamped around his wrist. She followed his gaze and swiftly let go. He felt his heart sink a little and cursed himself.

"Well, thanks again."

"I'll see you around, Kiara."

He walked out of the room and closed the door behind him, feeling a guilty, strange happiness.

10

KIARA'S ANNOYANCE WITH her mother only grew in the days that followed. In light of the battle, whose casualties had gone up to five, the training had been intensified, leaving her with no time to wallow in her feelings, or even to decide what it was that she was feeling. Anjali had appointed Krish and Aidan as the trainers-in-charge of the eighty-nine people in Ordenia who required training: newly-Turned fledgelings, people with jobs that didn't require training in combat and even the humans who worked in Ordenia as cleaners and chefs.

Ordenia often employed humans to run errands, clean, cook and perform other mundane activities. They were paid handsomely for their services and discretion.

"Listen up, everyone," Aidan called from the front of the room one morning, his voice commanding and authoritative. His eyes sparkled in the sunlight.

"Today," Krish said, his hand on Aidan's shoulder, "we'll focus on punching."

Kiara withheld a grin. The idea of her punching someone gave her immense satisfaction. But as it turned out, she was not as good at hitting punching bags as she was at smashing in Krish's face.

Krish observed her disapprovingly. "Sharma, I thought you were better than that," he said. He approached her punching bag. "Think of this as a way to relieve yourself," he started. Kiara raised a questioning brow.

"All right," he said, and scrunched up his face, as if searching for a memory. One seemed to surface, and his face went white with rage. He let out a guttural growl as his fist met the bag, the echo vibrating throughout the room. He then winked at Kiara, his eyes victorious. "Your turn, Kie. Think of something that makes your blood curl."

It didn't take long. The mere fact that she was a Katrol, the sheer unfairness of it all, made her unbelievably angry.

"Good," Krish said, reading her eyes like a familiar book. "Now I want you to feel it–" she fisted her palms, fire in her veins, fire that felt scarily real "–and hit."

She hit. She hit with such force that her knuckles weren't the only things that split. The punching bag lay on the floor, its rope severed by the sheer intensity of Kiara's anger. She smiled.

Aidan spotted Amara in the library as he was making his way to the training room.

She looked awful. Her hair was a rumpled mess, her eyes red and droopy. She sat, surrounded by a pile of books, head buried in a particularly chunky volume. So engrossed was she that she didn't notice him coming in.

"What are you reading?" he asked, leaning in to see the book she was hunched over.

Amara hastily slammed the book shut and batted her eyelashes at him, in the way she always did when she was hiding something.

"It's nothing. Just research for history lessons."

"Cut the crap–history lessons! Let me see that," he said, pointing at the book.

"Why? No, let go!" she protested, as he pulled it from her strong grip.

"*A Beginner's Guide to Katrols: Volume 5*?" he read out loud. "You've read four volumes before this? Why are you researching Katrols?"

A guilty shadow crossed over her face. "It's–"

"–nothing?" Aidan guessed, starting to scowl.

"Fine, I'll tell you, but you may not like what I say ... you have to promise to at least hear me out."

Aidan's scowl deepened, but he said, "Yes, okay."

"It says here that some of the insane strength and fighting skills that Katrols have in their werewolf form transfer to their human counterpart as well. It says that a Katrol, no matter their age, could fight against two or even three fully-grown and highly skilled regular wolves, and win. I think the people that attacked us were Katrols. We outnumbered them, and they still managed to do solid damage."

"That's good work, Mary," he said, patting her on the back.

She smiled faintly. "And I was thinking ... that's the reason Kiara outperformed Krish on her first day here."

"Makes sense."

"And I was also thinking how strange it was that–that so soon after Kiara's arrival, Ordenia was attacked for the first time in years," she continued, averting her gaze.

"So?"

"Aidan, I know you want to think the best of everyone, but isn't this too much of a coincidence to overlook? There has to be some kind of connection here. Maybe she's working for them.

Or maybe they want to recruit her or—I don't know. But there's something here, you can't deny it."

Aidan didn't know what to think. That Kiara would be a spy for an army of Katrols was a little far-fetched. Something flashed in his mind, uninvited—Kiara's large brown eyes, her weak smile, his hands on her waist ... he couldn't possibly believe she was evil.

Amara was just making things up, delusional and blinded by her hatred and need for revenge. Logic countered him and fought through his denial. Amara was intelligent; she was a good person. She knew how important Kiara was to Krish; she wouldn't blame her unless she was certain. Besides, her argument was very convincing. The evidence was too overwhelming. The odds of the attack being a coincidence were very small.

Aidan clutched his head with his hands as his thoughts warred among themselves:

Kiara can't be evil ...

How well do you really know her?

It's Kiara; she's Krish's best friend.

She's a Katrol. A monster.

She seems so—human.

Seems? Are you really going to base everything on 'seems'?

But she can't be ...

But what if she is?

But I feel—Oh, don't be stupid, Aidan. Your feelings don't matter right now. Admit it, you're just reluctant because you know Amara could be right. You know Kiara could be a spy. You just don't want it to be true.

If Amara was right and Kiara was the spy—God forbid— Aidan could finally quench his thirst for vengeance. He'd sleep in peace at night for the first time in months. His dreams wouldn't be haunted by the memory of Laura, reminding him that he needed to find out who was behind her murder, and rip out their throat with his own hands. He'd have ensured that the person responsible was gone, and that would give him peace and satisfaction like he'd never felt before.

Amara examined his face carefully, getting a glimpse of every haunting emotion he was experiencing. Aidan didn't know if he'd punch or thank himself later for what he was about to do.

He pulled up a chair next to Amara, picked up *Volume 6* and said, "How can I help?"

11

KIARA TRAINED VIGOROUSLY for the next two weeks, putting her heart and soul into every punch, kick and bout. Krish saw the exhaustion on her face, like on many others', and decided to give everyone the weekend off to kick back and let their bodies rest.

"Krish?" Kiara called as everyone dispersed. He glanced at her and wrapped up the conversation he was having with Aidan. He saw Aidan acknowledge Kiara's presence as well, and catch a breath before giving her a pained smile. Was that a hint of ... guilt on his face as he walked away?

"What's up, Sharma?" Krish asked, turning towards his friend.

"I, um, I know this is a bizarre request, but ..."

"What do you need?"

"Art supplies," she blurted out.

"Oh," Krish said, surprised.

"I mean, I understand if that's not possible, and you don't have to get me premium things but–"

"It feels like a part of you is missing?" Krish finished softly.

"Exactly," she said. Her voice quiet as she continued, "This ... all of this," she said, gesturing at their surroundings, "it's insane. It's only been three weeks since my birthday, and everything's moving so quickly. I just need something from my old life. I need to have a taste of normalcy."

He patted her cheek gently. "I'll make sure you have what you need before you wake up tomorrow." Krish knew that it was little things like this that touched Kiara in a way she couldn't explain. He saw the gratitude in her eyes, so he smiled and said, "Don't mention it. And yes, I *am* the best."

Krish was a man of his word. Kiara awoke the next day and opened her door to find a large package awaiting her. Drowsiness forgotten, she grabbed the huge cardboard box and ripped off the note.

Morning, Sharma, it read. *Got the best stuff I could find. Enjoy. Krish*

P.S: Included a little surprise. You're welcome.

"Krish, you beautiful human," Kiara whispered as she set the note aside and began opening the box. She stifled a scream when she peeked at the contents. Paint–more colours and shades than she had dared to dream of–a sketchpad, brushes, a huge palette, a bottle of water, a bowl and a huge box of charcoal stared back at her. She hugged the supplies to her chest, as if greeting old friends. She shrieked as she found her phone and headphones in the container as well. She peeled the plastic off the sketch pad and inhaled the wonderful scent of new paper. Quickly, she grabbed the hair-tie on her wrist and pulled her hair back into a ponytail, put on some music at full-blast and jammed her headphones into her ears. Putting her phone in the front pocket of her overalls, she got to work.

She painted her mother, curvy and elegant, her expression hard and determined, eyes shining with resolve and excitement as she commandeered the entire population of her sect at Ordenia. She sketched Advik, his eyes narrowed in concentration as his leg hit the dummy he practised on. Sweat beaded his forehead and drenched his tank top as he delivered the blow. Even though he was undergoing strenuous exercise, the ghost of a smile danced on his lips.

Then she made a drawing of Aidan, and another drawing of Aidan, and another, and another–she couldn't stop.

She drew Aidan as he held her hand and taught her how to use a bow, and shivered as she remembered the feeling of his breath on her neck, his whispered instructions, his fingers brushing back her hair, his hand on her face a few moments longer than it should have been ...

She drew Aidan as he hugged her excitedly after she had managed to hit the bull's eye. She remembered him whooping and sweeping her up in his arms, his lips a hair's breadth away from hers ...

She drew Aidan returning to Ordenia with a newly Turned boy, his arms tightly gripping the eighteen-year-old, eyes shining in satisfaction, lips curled into a half smile. The sunlight bouncing off his black hair and handsome face, making his cheekbones stand out even more than usual. He was touched that Kiara had been worried about him, and teased her about it relentlessly.

Kiara almost didn't have control over her body and mind as her brush flew across the pages, recreating her memories of Aidan over and over again, like a lovesick schoolgirl. She didn't even realize how much it drained her until the morning after, when she woke up in her overalls, body covered in paint and brush still tucked behind her ear.

There hadn't been any attacks on Ordenia in the last twenty-three days, but everyone had been training hard. As their trainer, Krish was really happy and proud with their progress. Those whose strength wasn't fighting were given other jobs—but nobody sat idle, everyone did their bit. Everybody had been given basic training by Krish, including Anjali, some high-ranking officers, and all the staff members.

"Krish?" Kiara called. He blinked out of his reverie.

"Yeah?"

"I think the training's going well. It's giving me an outlet for my anger and confusion, and I just ... thank you."

"I know. Anytime." She gave him a small smile and turned to leave. "Hold up. I'll have to run this by your mother, but I'm sure she won't mind. And according to the records ..." He opened a document on the computer system in the weapons room. "So ... the next full moon's the day after tomorrow."

Kiara tensed.

"And I'm not going to lie to you, it won't be easy. But, before that, do you maybe want to visit Mumbai again? Your father, Rish, Hritik ... I mean, you haven't seen them in so long and it might be good for you—oof!" All the breath was knocked out of his body as Kiara threw herself at him.

"Thank you, thank you, thank you," she whispered into his chest. "Though how can I just walk up to dad, Hritik and Rish after having vanished for the last month?"

"Meet me in the evening, outside the headquarters, at five. Today will be your last lesson, and it'll answer this question for you."

She smiled, but there was a little sadness in her eyes, and he understood it perfectly. Coaching her had been a wonderful and empowering journey. He had loved the experience and learnt so much from it. He had learnt to be patient, but to keep going; to be motivating and also to push her boundaries and, most of all, to make sure he was capable of keeping his best friend sane, and safe, during the challenges they will face.

Kiara needed a shower. She was flushed and sweaty from the day's training, and had taken the last couple hours off to bathe and relax before her final lesson with Krish. She took off her shoes and shrugged off her jacket. Looking at her arms properly for the first time since getting here, she nearly gasped.

Her arms had always been bony and skinny, but now she could see muscles tracing across her arms. She walked to the bathroom and stood in front of the mirror. She gawked. Her body had changed immensely since becoming a werewolf. Any softness she had, any amount of fat, had disappeared. She was leaner now, more athletic. Her hair had grown a little longer, and it was beautiful. She stared at her face. Nothing had really changed there, but she looked a lot more grown up. She definitely *felt* more grown up and mature, though the little sparkle she has always had in her brown eyes was alive as ever.

She smiled, and the girl staring back at her did, too.

12

AIDAN ALMOST GAVE his and Amara's investigation away. He knew he had been acting strange around Kiara ever since he had joined hands with Amara. He couldn't help it: the part of him that thought she was innocent felt hopelessly guilty for spying on her and taking advantage of her friendliness, but the part of him that suspected her bubbled with white-hot rage.

And then there was the third part of him that felt ... things around her. There would be moments where she was laughing, or deep in thought, or back from a training session, sweaty and exhausted, when he would look over and think: *God, she's beautiful.* Then there were times when she would look into his eyes, her gaze raw and challenging, and heat would flood through his body as he stared back.

Snap out of it, he would tell himself repeatedly as he looked away from her, heart deflating in the absence of the intensity of her stare. He wondered if he was the only one who felt like he was wronging her.

One afternoon, Aidan and Amara sat in the library, poring over volume after volume of *A Beginner's Guide to Katrols.*

"Mary?" Aidan said.

"Hmm?"

"Is there–is there a part of you that feels guilty about all this? Do you wonder if what we're doing is wrong?"

"No," she replied without hesitation.

"No?" he echoed.

"No," she said firmly. "Aidan, we're doing this for Laura. Look, there's a chance that Kiara is behind these attacks. If that's the case, we bust her, avenge Laura and save Ordenia." She sounded too sure and convinced for Aidan's comfort.

"And if she isn't?"

Amara inhaled deeply as she snapped her laptop shut and grabbed Aidan's hand. "If she isn't, I guess she'll have to understand."

"Oh, really?" said a voice. "Will I have to *understand*?"

Aidan's heart dropped to his stomach as Kiara emerged from behind a bookcase. Hurt and betrayal were etched on her face.

"Kiara!" Amara said. "Hi! What are you doing here?"

"Save the niceties, Amara, for someone you're not spying on!" Kiara spat. "You think I didn't notice you being extra nice to me, following me around, prying for details, trying desperately to get your hands on my phone, or on security tapes for everywhere I've been over the past few weeks?" She reached into her pocket and threw some tapes at Amara. "There," she snarled as Amara caught them. "Your damn security tapes, and here's my phone. Go ahead, I've already unlocked it. I won't be here when you're ready to apologize."

Amara was dumbstruck, all composure shattered.

"And you," she said, turning to Aidan, her voice soft, broken. "Was it all just an act? Did you use our f-friendship to spy on me, Aidan?" He flinched as though she'd slapped him. "I trusted you," she continued, the tears in her eyes finally spilling over. "I let you in. You–" She broke off, trying to compose herself.

"I can't do this anymore. I can't. I hope you're pleased with yourselves. My training ends today, and I'm leaving, going back to Mumbai. I–I'm not coming back. I don't know what I'll do, or where I'll go, but I'm not coming back. If even you two–Krish's best friend and girlfriend–can't trust me, who will? And the worst part is, I had no say in any of this. It's not my fault that some insatiable creature came after me–a creature you and all of Ordenia are supposed to be on the hunt for!"

"Kiara, I–"

"Save it, Amara. This is goodbye. I hope you got what you wanted. I don't want to hear from either of you, ever again." She turned on her heels and ran out of the library.

Aidan and Amara stared at each other. Then Aidan scrambled up and sprinted after Kiara. He thought she would've run to her room, but she hadn't been able to make it. He found her only a few feet away, collapsed on the floor, her body racking with silent sobs. He couldn't understand what she was muttering to herself.

"Kiara?" he said.

She turned her face to him, cheeks wet, eyes swollen.

"What do you want?" she said fiercely. "You know what–it doesn't matter. I don't care." She gathered herself and stood. "Just leave me alone."

He grabbed her wrist. "Kiara, I–"

"Let me be, Aidan."

"Kiara, just listen to me once."

"Aidan, I said, let GO!" She glared at him and flung his hand away. He winced sharply as his palm burnt where she'd touched him. He stared at Kiara's hand and saw the hint of a flame.

Her eyes widened in horror. "Just ... stay away," she stammered and bolted away from him.

This time, he didn't follow.

As he made his way to his room, he finally realized what Kiara had been murmuring to herself.

I'm a monster. I'm a monster. I'm a monster.

13

KIARA FURIOUSLY WIPED the tears away from her face. She had to see Krish for her last lesson in half an hour, and she knew that even the slightest hint of sadness on her face would upset and worry him. She certainly couldn't let him see her in her current state. Kiara washed her face and inspected her reflection in the mirror. She was surprised to see that her eyes had returned to their usual state, all signs of her encounter with Amara and Aidan gone.

She met Krish outside his room and, to her surprise, he led her back to the box-like room he'd locked her in not so long ago.

"Repaired the window, huh?" Kiara asked, trying to grin.

Krish grinned back. "For centuries now," he began, closing the door behind him, "us werewolves have hidden our existence from humans, but it proved impossible to do without some, uh–" he hesitated.

"Some what?" she asked curiously.

"Some magic."

"O-okay," she said. She had tried not to notice the signs of magic she'd seen ever since she had turned. She knew, of course, that the mere fact that werewolves existed was, well, magic, but the whole concept had somewhat scared her.

"Magic is a very broad term. There is different magic used by werewolves, by vampires–"

"What–vampires?"

"No one's seen one around for centuries, of course. But I like to believe they still exist."

"Of course you do," she muttered under her breath.

"What's that now?"

"Nothing," she said quickly.

"So, as I was saying, there's only a certain kind of magic werewolves have access to. As you have learnt, us wolves have always had an aptitude for and interest in potion-making. But that's not exactly *us* performing magic. It's just the ingredients that are magical; the overall process is quite mundane. One of the things we *can* do, though, is make ordinary people see what we want them to."

She arched her eyebrows at him.

"Now, for example, you want to make Hritik, Rish, your dad and schoolteachers believe that you have been among them for the past couple weeks, right?" He paused and she nodded. "You have to imagine what it would be like if you had actually been among them all this time. Imagine what it would've been like if you'd never Turned, or met your mother, or Amara and Aidan. Can you do that?"

At the mention of Amara and Aidan, her eyes glassed over. She turned away so that Krish wouldn't notice.

"I can do that," she said, picturing her pre-birthday self. The girl who would disappear in her room for hours, with her music, paint and a canvas, and come out with paint splattered all over herself, a stunning piece of art and a proud smile on her face. Kiara thought of the teenager who had lived motherless for years, but had an incredible father and a group of friends who she loved more than anything. She created a mental image of the weird but caring daughter who loved reading her dad's books, who was a creative thinker and an optimistic soul. The girl who had vanished without a trace since she'd arrived at Ordenia.

She looked at Krish. "I've got it. What now?"

"I want you to channel every last ounce of your strength into that image."

She squeezed her eyes shut and forced every last inch of her being into the picture–everything was fine, she was with her friends, she would go home to her dad's awesome cooking and comical innocence, to a regular life in Mumbai.

She opened her eyes slowly and gaped as she stared ahead at what she'd done. There was a swirling, glowing orb in front of her, inside which was a display of everything she had just envisioned.

She looked sideways at Krish, and he smiled and spoke in a gentle voice, "Good job, Sharma. Now, you have to will it towards me. Into my brain. Come on."

It took every last morsel of her energy and concentration to direct this magical object that her mind had created into her best friend. She saw Krish stagger back slightly as if he was being propelled by an invisible wave, to land lightly on his feet again.

"Krish, are you okay? Did I do it right?"

He nodded proudly and caught her just as her knees buckled from the effort. He offered to carry her to her room, and as much as she wanted him to, her pride got in the way. But he might as well have, for she leant heavily on him all the way. He helped her to her bed, walked out of the room and came back with a box of doughnuts. Her stomach growled loudly as she took two, grinning. Krish looked highly amused as he helped himself.

"Oh my God," Kiara breathed, her mouth full. "It's over." When he said nothing, she continued, "Krish, what happened to you when I did that whole magic memory ball thing?"

"I just saw everything that you had envisioned. A human's mind would force them to believe whatever was in the Memory Orb. Not magic memory ball thing."

"So can I do this to anyone?" she asked.

"As long as they're in your line of sight," he replied. They took a few bites of their doughnuts in silence. "After you come back tomorrow," he said, "you and I need to talk about what you're going to do next."

"Right," she said, "after I come back."

"I suggest you catch a few hours of sleep before you leave. And hey, your face looks like you tripped and fell into a puddle of horseshit."

"Hey!"

"Clean up is all I'm saying. You look ghastly with all that brown stuff on you."

She pushed him out of the room and slammed the door in his face.

Kiara was falling through a dark abyss.

Flames suddenly erupted around her, engulfing her. She screamed for Krish in agony. But how would he hear her scream if she couldn't? Why wasn't he here yet? What was happening to her? A sudden wave crashed against her and sent her sprawling to her side. She coughed up water and gasped for breath. She noticed she lay on a grassy shore. She reached out to feel the familiar, soft grass, but the blade wrapped itself around her throat. She gagged and choked. Her vision blurred. Her mind raced. So this was how she was going to die? Choked to death by a blade of grass, for hell's sake? A deep gurgling sound in her throat was all the laughter she could manage. A strong gust of wind pulled her off her feet, and then she was falling again, falling through a black abyss. Something was shaking her. It was the wind again.

"Kiara? Kiara!"

Since when did the wind speak? And why did it sound so familiar? Why did the panicked voice instil fear in her heart?

"It's just a dream!"

Yeah, Kiara told herself, it's just a dream. The wind can't speak.

"Come on, stay with me."

She didn't want to stay with it. She wanted it to let her go. How would she let it know? She could tell it. She would tell it.

"Let. GO!" she screamed. It was the shock of hearing her own voice that pried her eyes open. A concerned set of black eyes swam into her vision. Eyes she would know anywhere.

"Krish," she breathed.

"That's right, Kie," he said, his voice thick with relief. His eyes assessed her face. "You–you look pale–scary pale. You know what, you don't have to go now, we can always reschedule," he rambled on.

"I'm going," she said fiercely, composing herself.

"Are you sure?"

"I'm going," she repeated.

He gave her a stern look. She glared back.

"Well then," he said, settling himself comfortably on her bed. "Let's go over the details of your trip. Your dad will be out on his fishing trip so you'll have to meet him another time."

Kiara's heart sank a little. She had been looking forward to seeing her father again.

"Now, you're going to spend the night at Hritik and Rishika's place, I assume?"

She nodded. She had called Rishika up a couple of days ago and she had immediately agreed. As far as she was aware, they did not know of the werewolves or Ordenia.

"Okay," he said, and hesitated. "I just feel like there's something about your trip that's not right. I can't put my finger on it, though. The Memory Orbs can be exhausting the first few times, so I've taken care of that. I've checked and re-checked the date of the full moon on every server I could get my hands on, I've got everything planned down to the last minute, I've taken express permission from every authority I could think of–"

"Hey, hey." She took his hand. "I'll be okay. I promise."

"Well then, you should have this." He took off the watch from around his wrist and fastened it on hers. "This is only given to people going on seriously dangerous missions. I had it when I went to get you. This here," he pointed to a small red button on the left corner of the watch, "will alert Ordenia and we'll send immediate backup–"

"Backup?" Kiara laughed. "I'm just going to meet some friends, Krish."

"Truth is," Krish sighed, "I had to pull a lot of strings and call in quite a few favours to make this trip happen. The Alphas are not happy at all. They refused, point blank, to send you at my request, but then your mom stepped in and there was a huge argument ... what I'm trying to say is, no one's taking chances here, Kiara."

"Thank you so much."

"Anytime. Just–be okay. I'll see you soon."

Not trusting herself to speak, she smiled and nodded at him.

Kiara reached Hritik and Rishika's early that evening. She swallowed a wince as she hugged Rish, the latter's silver necklace boring into the former's skin. The evening flew by as normally as it used to earlier, and soon enough it was sunset.

The three of them decided to set up camp outside the house. They changed into their nightclothes and made plans to roast marshmallows over a campfire. Their goal was to replicate the summer camp they had had in the woods when they were younger. It was a silly, childish thing for a group of people in their late teens to do, but they'd been doing it for too long to care.

Outside, Kiara smiled contentedly, grateful that all was going well. She glanced at the night sky and saw the full moon shining bright. That's when all hell broke loose.

14

KRISH WAS INFURIATED. "So, you spied on her?" he yelled at Amara and Aidan, not for the first time. He glared at them, and when Aidan opened his mouth to say something, he burst out, "Yes, go on, Aidan. What can you say that will possibly justify your actions?"

"Nothing," Amara said. She looked, and sounded, absolutely miserable. "Look, don't blame Aidan. It's my fault. It's all my fault. I didn't trust Kiara. I dragged him into this. I–"

"But I agreed to help you," Aidan cut in. "Krish, it's my fault. I could've dissuaded her, I could have stopped this before it even started. I am to blame. I–"

"This is all very touching," Krish said through gritted teeth. "But what the hell, guys?"

He knew that even though they were horribly wrong, they could have justified themselves. They could have said that everything lined up, that it was too much of a coincidence. They could have said that after Laura, they couldn't be around Katrols, couldn't trust them ever again. They could have said a million things, but they just stared at their shoes in silence. Aidan mumbled something.

"What's that now?" Krish demanded.

"I checked her phone," Amara blurted out, "and the security footage. It–it checks out."

Krish threw up his hands. "Of course it does!" he said, exasperated. Then he turned to Aidan. "What were you saying?"

"Kiara's not–" Aidan broke off and shook his head. "She's not coming back."

"What?"

"Krish, I'm so, so sorry–"

"Well, that doesn't bring back my best friend, now, does it?" Krish thundered, before storming out.

"Where are you going?" Amara called after him.

"I'm going to find her."

"No, you're not."

He rounded on her. "Amara–"

She flinched but held her ground. "You're not going to find her. She's incredibly upset right now, courtesy of us, and the last thing she needs tonight is to be with a werewolf, even if it's you. She needs to have a mundane evening with her human friends. She'll be much better off for it."

As much as he wanted to, Krish couldn't disagree with her. He yanked his sleeve out of her grip and growled, "First thing in the morning, I'm going to find her."

He slammed the door behind him as he left.

Aidan and Amara sat in silence. "We shouldn't have," Amara whispered, her eyes swimming in tears. "Oh God, what was I thinking?"

You were thinking of Laura, Aidan thought miserably. He was remembering how he'd given Kiara archery lessons, moving her soft hair away from her face as she held the bow, their faces nearly touching. Her lips were a quarter of an inch away from his, and the need to close the space between them almost overwhelmed him. He recalled scooping her up in his arms, using her bull's eye shot as an excuse to hold her close. He recalled the concern on her face as he returned with a newly Turned eighteen-year-old boy. Her face had broken out into a wide smile, and he thought it was the most beautiful thing he'd ever seen. And now he'd probably never get to see it again. He put his head in his hands.

Suddenly, Amara sat bolt upright. "We should bring her back."

"What?"

"Kiara. We should bring her back. We should go talk to her tomorrow morning, apologize, convince her to come back. It's the least we can do."

Aidan nodded in agreement. "We can track her scent. And we know what Hritik and Rishika look like. We'll find her."

They watched the sun set in silence. Then the moon arose, and Aidan stared at it in shock. The full moon wasn't until the next night! How had they got the calculation wrong? Before he could give it more coherent thought, he doubled over into a familiar crouch. His palms turned to paws, hair grew into fur and mouth elongated into a snout. He heard his clothes ripping as his body expanded. He was sure his eyes were now a sparkling green.

He stared at wolf-Amara next to him. Her features contorted with horror. The same realization hit him a second later.

Kiara.

Aidan urged his paws to carry him as fast as they could, Amara on his heels. They leapt out of Aidan's room and made their way to Kiara's to find a piece of clothing they could use to track her. When they arrived, someone was already there, tearing through her closet, wildly rummaging through her possessions. The wolf turned his head to acknowledge Aidan and Amara. Krish.

Aidan was always amazed at how werewolves recognized each other in their wolf forms, but there was somehow a stark resemblance between human-Krish and wolf-Krish.

Amara pawed at Krish's stark white furred limb. *Aidan and I can take care of this. You stay here.*

She then widened her eyes and let out a whine. *Please.*

Krish eyed the pair of them suspiciously, his green eyes flitting between them. Finally, he let out a reluctant growl, but his eyes held a deeper message. *Fine, go.* But *please make sure she's okay.*

Amara licked Krish's face and while he didn't reciprocate, he didn't push her away either.

Aidan lunged for Kiara's closet and was almost overwhelmed by the scent of her. He forced himself to concentrate and grabbed her favourite green shirt. Amara nudged him hard. *Let's go. Now.*

Aidan couldn't agree more.

Amara ran like she'd never run before, her dark grey fur swishing in the wind. Her paws galloped over solid ground, leaving dust in their wake. Aidan was right at her side, Kiara's shirt clutched in his mouth.

Kiara.

Guilt catalyzed her speed. Faster than she thought possible, they reached the gate to Ordenia–the barrier between the ordinary and the magical, the safe and the dangerous.

This was the first time Amara and Aidan had ventured into Mumbai, but they had no time to explore. Tracking Kiara's scent was simple, instinctual to the wolves.

Amara knew they were too late long before they'd arrived at Rishika's house. Out in the yard, they found Rishika cowering under a small tent, its flaps open. Amara looked around and saw Hritik lying facedown a few feet away, surrounded by a pool of blood.

Dead.

Kiara had killed him. And unless Amara and Aidan found her first, she would kill them, too.

PART 2

15

AMARA AND AIDAN split up to scout the surroundings. Big tree, big tree, big tree and another big tree. Rishika seemed to have run out from under the tent and was now sobbing behind one of the trees. Quiet, stifled sobs, but Amara's wolf ears caught the sound. She circled back to the spot where she'd left Aidan. He emerged from a cluster of trees behind the house, majestic paws moving gracefully. She raised her head in question, and he shook his. Nothing.

Where was Kiara? Amara cast her eyes over her surroundings once again: trees, bushes, Rishika clutching her necklace and weeping softly, more trees, bushes, greenery—

Amara did a double take. Rishika's necklace. Of course, taking out two birds with one stone. Her head full of apologies, she pounced.

What are you doing, Mary? Aidan thought, not for the first time. Amara had just thrown herself at Rishika. The poor girl screamed hysterically as she wriggled under Amara's grip. They struggled together for a few minutes. Then Amara jumped away, and Rishika ran for her life.

Aidan lifted a cautious yellow paw before putting it on the ground as he made his way to Amara sceptically. She was grimacing. She pointed to the floor. A glint of silver winked at Aidan. Understanding dawned upon him. He nodded at Amara. Somehow, they already knew their roles—Aidan would continue to hunt for Kiara while Amara guarded their weapon.

There was a sudden rustling of leaves behind Aidan. He turned quickly and heard a low growl as he stared, transfixed in horror, at the monster Kiara had become.

Her brown fur was matted and sticky with gore. Her claws were red, the horrible, metallic stench of blood thick in the night air. She roared, revealing jagged, maroon teeth. Was that ... an arm she was carrying? Was she eating it? Her crimson eyes betrayed nothing.

She suddenly sprang out and lunged. Aidan rolled sideways to dodge the blow. She swiped her paw at him, he deflected not a second too soon. She bared her teeth. He bared his. She jumped on him, and he hit the ground painfully, gritting his teeth to keep from growling in pain. She towered over him victoriously and bit into his limb, ripping open his flesh. Blood gushed out. Aidan couldn't help it then—he howled. His fur turning dirty with his own thick blood. Kiara hovered back for a moment, and he took advantage of her hesitation. She thudded to the earth. Aidan managed to pull himself up and limp-ran towards Amara. Kiara followed a moment later, her speed unparalleled. Aidan knew that he would've been flattened if Amara hadn't jumped out from behind a bush and onto Kiara when she did. Amara held down Kiara and gestured to the necklace. Aidan braced himself but wasn't prepared for the sharp stab of pain that raced through his already-aching body. He fought the urge to fling the necklace away as he limped back to Kiara, and let out a sigh of relief as he transferred it to her front limb. She roared—a guttural, wild noise. Her cries tore through the beautiful silence of the night. Amara had climbed on top of her, but wouldn't last much longer as she was pressing down the silver onto Kiara. Aidan would have two unconscious girls to carry back.

He tore off a chunk of a nearby bush to replace Amara's paw. He climbed onto Kiara's giant mass, placed the bush on her body and pressed on it. After what felt like an eternity, Kiara stilled. Aidan and Amara exchanged looks of disbelief and relief. Aidan snatched up the blanket that Kiara and her friends had used for the tent. Amara tried to help, but he snarled at her to stay back. She'd already exerted herself a great deal that night. The silver she had held down on Kiara for way longer than he could have had wounded her hands gravely.

Once the blanket was securely around Kiara, Aidan sank his teeth into it and lifted. Amara followed him, a few paces slower than she usually was.

They were making their way to the heart of the forest, carrying Kiara, when suddenly, a sharp beeping noise made Aidan jump. Amara whined hopelessly. She had accidentally stepped on the watch Krish had given Kiara, which meant that any second ...

Aidan knew he couldn't have kept Hritik's death a secret from Ordenia for too long, but the last thing he wanted was for them to find out like this—blood everywhere, disfigured body parts scattered in the forest. A familiar howl pierced the air. Advik, followed by four senior wolves, had arrived. It was too late.

Aidan flew through the forest, the wind howling in his ears and whipping across his face. He hastily deposited Kiara onto the floor and sought out the whispers of the magic. His eyes burned for a second, and the door formed in front of his eyes. He yanked at the doorknob with his mouth and threw it open. He picked up the blanket Kiara was wrapped in and ran a few steps forward into Ordenia. What he saw made his jaw drop.

Kiara rolled onto the floor.

A fierce battle was raging, and there was blood everywhere. They had been attacked again, and he could tell who the enemy was by looking at their red eyes—Katrols. The fur on some of their lithe bodies was covered in the blood of their opponents. One brown furred wolf glared at Aidan and Amara, observing the limp girl splayed on the floor. It started to come towards them, but stumbled onto the ground as a magnificent black wolf with yellow eyes pounced on it.

And they seemed perfectly in control ... Aidan's head spun. He turned cluelessly to Amara, who was behind him, and she let out what might have been a sob.

16

KIARA JOLTED AWAKE. Her hands and feet were bound by chains. She was lying on a soft mattress in a room she had been locked in before, during the first battle. She inspected the room as far as her shackles would allow–same white cupboards, same desolate, lifeless interior. She was startled to notice she was wearing clothes she had never seen before. She turned her palms over to see they were coated in something that looked horribly like blood. She bit back a scream as sweat ran down her spine, causing goosebumps to erupt all over her skin.

"Krish?" She called out in a panicky voice. "Advik, Aish, Aidan? Is anybody there?"

"Mumma?" she half-sobbed as the door flew open.

It was Aisha who walked in. Kiara swallowed back her relief when she saw her friend's expression, dread pooling in her gut instead. Aisha looked–there was no other word for it–murderous. Her eyes brimmed with unshed tears of fury. She visibly shook with rage. Her mouth was pressed into a thin line.

Kiara froze in shock as the other girl knelt to face her, leant in and whispered, "This is for Hritik."

"For Hritik?" Kiara exclaimed. "Aisha, what ..."

Aisha smirked. Then, very slowly, she pulled out a dagger from her belt. Kiara struggled against the chains, but their hold on her was impregnable.

Aisha grabbed her face with one hand and slowly sliced her cheek open with the other.

"I know you don't believe in God," Kiara rasped, as pain shot through her and blood ran down her chin, "but no higher power will forgive you for this."

"Why don't you ask them for me?" Aisha shot back.

Kiara bit Aisha's hand, hard. The other girl yelped and swore as Kiara arched her knee upwards with such force that Aisha fell backwards. Kiara had just enough time to let out a cry for help, when she saw Advik bolting in.

Advik quickly pulled out a throwing star from his belt and hurled it into Kiara's outstretched palm. Kiara caught it clumsily, yelled, "Hey!" and aimed for Aisha's shoulder just as she turned around to look at her. She let it fly as fast as she could, but Aisha was quicker. She ducked and the star missed her by millimetres, thudding to the floor uselessly.

While Kiara helplessly looked around for a makeshift weapon with her hands tied, Advik swiftly flung a star at Aisha's back. "Bull's eye," he muttered as Aisha let out a sigh, crumpled to the floor and stopped moving. Advik didn't waste a moment. He strode towards Kiara and unfastened the chains. "Are you okay?"

"I'm good. Is she ... did you ..." Kiara started, pointing to Aisha.

"Kill her?" Advik finished for her. "God, no. That's a little something Amara and I have been working on. A tranquilizer star, if you will. The chemicals it is imbued with, on contact with the skin, make the receiver pass out."

"Thank God, she's alive." Kiara sighed and smiled wanly at Advik.

Advik had never been the sombre type, which resulted in no one ever taking him seriously. He hid it well, but she knew her childhood friend too well to not notice that it bothered him. Or that his eyes carried immeasurable sorrow in that moment.

Before she could enquire, he said, "She's been the spy all along."

"What?"

"She got into this room, a room that only your mother and her seniors have access to. She was there with me the day of the first attack. I bet it was her that knocked me out. And ..." He reached for her unconscious body and took something that was dangling from her pocket. Keys—at least thirty of them.

Advik shook his head, silver lining his dark eyes. "Not her too ..." he mumbled.

"What do you mean, 'too'?" Kiara's anxiety must have reflected on her face, because Advik pulled her close and ran his hands gently through her hair.

"Now, before I tell you, I want you to know that this is not your fault, by any means."

"You're scaring me, Advik. What happened?"

He hesitated before replying with a question of his own. "What's the last thing you remember?"

She thought hard. Memories blurred and flashed before her eyes. "I was visiting Rish and Hritik, but what does that have to do with anything? Why am I in chains? The last time I was shackled was when there was a full ..." She trailed off, horror knocking the wind out of her. "No."

A few moments of silence, horrible and eerie, followed. "Did Hritik and Rish make it out okay?" she finally asked in a small voice.

"Rish made it out," he said gently, cautiously.

"Hritik ...?" she whispered. It was all she could manage.

He reluctantly looked her in the eyes and shook his head with a finality that broke her heart. She buried her head in his shoulder as a sob tore through her, threatening to swallow her whole. The world swam in front of her watery eyes. Her crying grew hysterical. Advik held her tighter as she spiralled further and further, her heart throbbing so painfully she could almost feel it through her numb body.

She'd killed him. She'd killed Hritik.

"T–that's no–not all, is it?" she asked Advik between sobs.

"No," he answered, his voice quivering horribly. "The day Hritik–" He stopped himself, a shaky, dry sob escaping him. "The day it happened, there was another attack." She drew a breath. "Remember the theory Amara pitched a few weeks ago?"

Kiara nodded. Of course, she remembered. How could she not?

"An army of Katrols," Advik confirmed. "Red, glowing eyes, gigantic and–"

"Yes, Advik, I got it."

He shot her an apologetic glance.

"If they really were Katrols," Kiara mused, "how did they tell friend and foe apart? How did they know those they had to kill from their allies?"

"That part stumps us. We don't know."

Kiara's eyebrows quirked in suspicion. As if he could predict what she was going to say, he added, "But we are sure that they were Katrols. They're ten times more vicious than regular wolves. They're stronger, faster, bigger. Two of us could barely take on one of them. We almost died trying. Almost," he reassured her.

"What happened then? Was anyone hurt? Did we win?"

"About that ... something really weird happened, and no one can make sense of it," he said with a scowl.

"Weird," Kiara said, her voice thick with tears. "Tell me about it."

Advik attempted a smile, but it turned into a grimace. "We were losing horribly. In fact, it was such a disaster that we considered surrendering." Kiara shuddered. "Then ... Aidan and Amara came in with you in that–" he made some undecipherable gesture "–blanket roll thingy. And they just–they all backed off. They retreated and ran away. We don't know why they thought to leave after they saw you guys. But the decision to leave was unanimous. They didn't even look back at us."

Kiara swallowed hard. If she had apparently scared away an entire army of Katrols, she knew that she was too dangerous to live among people she loved. She looked at Advik sadly and squeezed his hand.

"We'll figure it out, okay?" *You will.* "And Advik, I ... I'm sorry I haven't been spending much time with you lately."

"Oh, that's all right. You've been busy with training and stuff."

"Yes, but I should've made an effort. I'm sorry."

He nodded. "We can make up for that."

She smiled slightly and got up to leave. "Just going to get some fresh air," she said in answer to his questioning look.

Apparently, she was a better actor than she gave herself credit for. She made a stop at the weaponry and scanned the room. Dawn sat on a wooden table at the centre of the room. She closed her hand around its familiar hilt and made her way rapidly towards the edge of the forest. She knew that even though Krish had given her his word that he'd kill her if she got too dangerous, he wouldn't be able to follow through with his promise.

Kiara turned back for one last glance of Ordenia. Faces and memories flashed through her mind. She would never hurt anyone else she loved.

With that as her last thought, she drew the dagger towards her own throat.

17

"STOP FUSSING, MARY. I'm fine." Aidan *was* fine. His arm throbbed a little, but it was nothing he couldn't handle. The wound had been cleaned, bandages applied. Amara stepped back.

"Sorry." Her voice was small.

"Do you ... blame her?"

Amara blanched. "I suppose I can't blame you for asking, can I?" She let out a bitter laugh. "No, of course not. I guess I've finally learned to separate Kiara from the Katrol."

Aidan nodded. "And Krish?"

"He's grieving. Not ready to talk about it yet, but he knows I'll be there when he does. Do you think she'll forgive us?"

He didn't have an answer so he shrugged on his jacket. "I need to be outside. Clear my head. You coming?"

"I'm coming."

Just as she was about to press the blade into her skin, Kiara heard a familiar voice.

"Kiara?" Aidan said. "Wha–" He looked from her to Dawn. His jaw hardened, his eyes betraying the shock and fear he was struggling to contain.

Amara, beside him, was not as good at hiding her panic. Her eyes widened fearfully and her lips started to quiver.

"Okay, Kiara," Aidan said in a calm voice. "I'm unarmed, okay?" He raised his arms over his head. Kiara noticed his shoulder was bandaged up and thought, *I did that.* "I'm coming to you. Please, just listen to me. Whatever happened, whatever you think you are, it's not true. It's not fair. You didn't choose to be a Katrol. You didn't choose any of this," he said, inching closer to her. "Now, please, just drop the dagger, Kiara. Please just drop it, and we'll figure it out together. I promise."

"How can you do that?"

"Do what?"

"*Lie* like that. Of course I didn't choose to be what I am, but these are the cards that were handed to me. This is what I am, what I'll always be. You investigated me, for God's sake!"

Amara and Aidan let out identical winces.

"I want to blame you, but how can I?" Kiara went on.

"I lost my sister," Amara whispered, "to a Katrol."

"Not helping," Aidan muttered so only she could hear him.

She shot him a look. "Laura. She came to my room one day and told me she'd found out the identity of the other Katrol. Before these attacks, we didn't know this army existed, and thought there were only two. I was only twelve at the time, and I didn't know to warn my sister against going after the Katrol on her own. She said she wanted to hunt it and bring it to Ordenia, and I had always known she'd overestimated herself, but I never thought it would lead to her death."

Aidan looked at her. It was the first time she'd used that word while talking about Laura.

"I've demonized your kind for too long. That side of you doesn't change the human you are. I can't promise you everything will be all right, I can't promise you won't hurt anyone else. But I promise it will get better. I'll make sure of it."

Dawn slipped out of Kiara's hand, and Aidan was quick to catch it. Amara pulled Kiara into a fierce hug, and the two girls wept in each other's arms. With her arms around Kiara's neck, Amara seemed to finally let go of Laura.

Little did she know that beside her, ducking to hide his tears, Aidan did, too.

18

"YOU WANTED TO see me, Mr Oberoi?" said Anjali Sharma. "Yes," Krish said, "I wanted to formally request that you allow me–and any of my friends who feel they can handle it–to be present at Aisha's trial today."

She looked a little surprised, but said, "Permission granted."

"The trial is scheduled for today," Krish announced in the cafeteria later. "And we are all allowed to attend it."

The following silence was deafening. It had been five days since Hritik's death. Kiara, Advik and Krish had attended his funeral, before which Advik had successfully altered Rishika's memory. As far as she knew, a rabid dog had attacked the three of them and killed her brother while Kiara had managed to save herself and flee.

There were clear signs of exhaustion and grief on all their faces. Krish looked pale and unkempt. Advik had dark circles under his red-rimmed eyes. Kiara knew that she herself looked like she hadn't eaten in days. All five of them had been dodging the thoughts of the consequences of Kiara's actions. Not just for her, but for Krish, Aidan and Amara, too.

"What–what will this interrogation entail?" Kiara asked, her voice hoarse from disuse. Under the table, Aidan squeezed her hand.

Advik spoke first. "Magic is a very ... obscure concept. And especially when it comes to us werewolves, it's very limited. Turning every month, conjuring Memory Orbs, getting burnt upon contact with silver. Perhaps Katrols have some more powers than the rest of us, but it doesn't really go further than that. The only other form of magic we get close to is substances. Magical elements. Potions, concoctions, serums–that sort of thing. And there's a truth serum we use for interrogations, one that was developed just a few months ago. It forces one to speak the truth."

"Okay, I guess that's not so bad then."

"No, Kiara. It *forces* you to speak the truth," Amara said.

"And if you refuse to talk, it ... hurts you," Krish finished.

Kiara winced. Aidan's grip on her hand had become painfully tight. She shot him a concerned glance, but decided she would investigate later.

After a few awkward moments of silence, Advik dug into his burger, moaning contentedly. They all stared at him.

"What?" he demanded, sending tiny bits of patty flying. "I'm not allowed to eat?"

Aidan and Krish exchanged a glance and shrugged, as if to say, *Fair enough.* They, too, started wolfing down their food.

A few minutes later, Hugo walked in, and Aidan paled visibly. Hugo was Anjali's right-hand man, and Kiara knew that he gave Krish nightmares. He was tall, pale and handsome to a fault. His chipped teeth made him all the more intimidating.

"You three," he barked at the boys, "interrogation room, now. Call them, too," he pointed at the girls, "if they can stomach it."

The interrogation room looked as if it had been pulled right out of a police precinct: three bare white walls and a glass one that was see-through. The investigators sat outside this enclosure, all staring at the subject intensely.

Aisha had always been small, but she'd never looked this breakable. Her body was chained to the grey chair that she sat on, and there were angry red marks on her hands and feet, as if she had resisted and struggled but failed to break free.

Krish's heart broke to see his childhood friend like that, but he didn't want her to see his grief, so he quickly arranged his expression into a blank and stony one.

Anjali Sharma sat in a sombre black suit next to Hugo. There were six other black-suited seniors in the chairs around her. Anjali watched her daughter enter the room and cleared her throat. Everyone fell silent.

"Aisha," Anjali began. "You are being held on trial for your attempted murder of Kiara Sharma. Is that right?" Aisha nodded. "Before we dissect that, have you ever done anything else to harm Ordenia, or anyone who resides here?"

Aisha appeared to be struggling as a whimper escaped her lips. "Yes," she spluttered finally, spitting out blood. Anjali straightened in her chair. Krish felt Kiara tense next to him.

"Talk us through it. Spare no detail."

"Hugo here was in charge before you were. You remember that, of course. And that meant brutality for the sake of brutality, injustice to teach us that the world is unfair and violence to impart the lesson that you will never survive out there if you're not a fighter," Aisha spat, the acid in her tone so evident that Amara flinched. "And it wasn't enough that you were battling mental illness, or family issues, or any other real-world problem. Unless you could pick up a goddamned weapon and cut someone to pieces, you had no value here. No purpose, no use. And what do you do with things that are not useful? Discard them."

"What does this have to do with anything, Ms Waters?" said Anjali.

"*Everything*. It's been so easy for your little girl." She turned to Kiara. "Lucky you. Your mother is the boss, your best friend is your mentor, you've found a group of people you fit in with. It's not this convenient for all of us, Kiara. My mentor was this girl named Surasha. She seemed nice enough in front of the officials. But she knew I was a Katrol the second I Turned, of course."

Krish heard Aidan exhale sharply.

"She didn't tell anyone. I was the first of my friends to Turn. I was alone here, and very impressionable. Back then, training was a longer process. More torturous, more strenuous. Surasha drilled into my head that no one cared about me. I resisted at first, of course. But when my second Turning came around, and no one noticed that I wasn't around, that I was in chains in a dirty, old basement, I knew Surasha had been right. I knew that you guys, humans, for all I knew, were no use to me in this world."

Advik made a funny noise at the word 'use'. Kiara blinked furiously and let go of Aidan's arm, which she had been clutching. Krish watched in surprise as Aidan winced and shifted, clutching the spot where Kiara's skin had been in contact with his mere seconds ago.

"Surasha got into my head. And not knowing any better, I let her in. She took me to this wonderful place, this place where we were all Katrols, roaming freely, without being hunted, without being hated. We were accepted because we were together. A community. A family."

Krish glanced at Kiara again. He didn't think he was imagining the look of yearning on his best friend's face.

"They're teaching me how to be ordinary. To be in control of myself when I Turn," she said, gazing intently at Kiara. "I'm willing to trade that information for my freedom and a clean slate."

Anjali looked torn.

"Mumma," Kiara spoke up. "You can't do this. You can't let her slip away just to cure me. Please."

For a moment Anjali looked like she wanted to argue, but instead said, "You heard her. We're not trading. Continue, please."

Aisha looked triumphant. "See, Kiara? They don't care about us. They don't understand what it's like–they'll never understand what it's like, living like this."

"It is my choice, Aisha," Kiara answered simply.

"Please continue," Anjali said, looking worried.

Aisha's lips seemed to force open against her will. "They gave me a home, a place to belong. Sure, I had to endure Hugo during the day, but at night, I was free. Aidan, you remember what Hugo was like, don't you?"

Aidan closed his eyes and took a deep breath. He was shaking all over.

Anjali said, "That is enough. One more statement that doesn't strictly pertain to my question, and you'll be at the mercy of Hugo's interrogation tactics again. Is that understood, Ms Waters?"

Genuine fear clouded Aisha's eyes. "Eventually, we started developing a thirst for power. Katrols were so clearly the most superior sect of the werewolf world, yet we were the ones being hunted down and oppressed. All of us, at some point or another, directly or indirectly, have been hurt by the actions of Ordenia. And you know the one thing that unites people more than anything else possibly can? It's not love. It's not friendship. It's hatred. The need for revenge unified us. So, we branded ourselves as the Uprising. We drew up a symbol." She pulled her shirt aside to reveal a mark on her collarbone.

"Malcolm," Anjali muttered. One from those assembled behind her rose and inspected the tattoo. He closed his eyes and conjured an Orb to project the symbol to the room. It was a wolf, with one green and one red eye. A silver dagger pierced through the green one, and the red one was surrounded by a ring of blood.

"What is this supposed to represent?"

"Oh, I think it's perfectly self-explanatory. The green-eyed wolves need to be put in their place. Using violence, if necessary. The blood around the Katrol's eye shows that we're willing to sacrifice some of our own for the greater good."

"And what is this 'greater good' that you speak of?" Anjali asked.

Aisha gawked at Anjali as if she were a fish with feathers. "Making sure Katrols are the hunters and not the hunted."

"How did Surasha fare?"

A wicked smile played on Aisha's lips. "Oh, she's gone. An accident, it was. A sacrifice for the greater good."

"A sacrifice for *your* good," Krish said through gritted teeth.

Aisha didn't deny it.

"And what exactly did you do for this organization?"

Completely unabashed, Aisha said, "I leaked classified information from here. It was me that knocked Advik out during the first battle so I could get access to some weapons to smuggle out. Advik had turned the security cameras off in case anyone unwanted was watching, bless his soul."

Amara laid a comforting hand on Advik's shoulder.

"Advik's little slip-up also made it possible for me to hack into your systems undetected. I summoned Anjali's guards away to break into her office and alter Ordenia's records of the full moon."

"So, your aim is to make Katrols dominate over all sects of werewolves at Ordenia–how? By eliminating all other werewolves?"

"Not so much eliminating as reducing to a significantly smaller number, something we can control. We only want as many of you alive as we need. You can surrender now, of course."

"What's your strength?" Anjali asked, as if Aisha hadn't said the last bit at all.

Aisha attempted to resist. It was brutal to watch. She clawed at her throat so hard that her nails left a trail of bloody scratches on her neck. Her eyes glossed over with unshed tears as she choked out, her voice rough and broken, "A hundred and sixty-seven before the attacks. Ordenia took four out."

Anjali bit her lip anxiously. The strength of Ordenia was two hundred and twenty-nine, but only two hundred and two were in fighting condition. And it took two of them to take down one Katrol. They were badly outnumbered.

"How many more of you are among us?"

"I don't know."

"What do you mean?"

"I don't know. To protect the identities of the members of the Uprising, we don't always know who may be working alongside us, should one of us be compromised. I don't even know who I'm working under. I just believe in the Uprising as a concept, and I have to see the Katrols succeed."

Aidan finally burst out, "Look, this is all fine, but why would your Uprising want Kiara dead? Shouldn't they be trying to, I don't know, recruit her or something?"

Anjali didn't reprimand him for speaking out of turn. In fact, she was shaking with fury herself. "Answer him."

"Oh, they didn't tell me to kill Kiara. They actually want that girl alive, for whatever reason. But this one, she's one of the most vile, unbeatable Katrols I've ever encountered. She killed Hritik."

"Shut up about Hritik," Krish said angrily, before he could stop himself. But Aisha just went on.

"None of the rest of you noticed when I was going through a hard time with my training, when I was horribly drained for months at a stretch, but despite being human, Hritik did. He noticed, he understood. The rest of you did nothing for me. He did. Aidan, you were in Ordenia for weeks before I arrived, but you didn't see my agony. Krish and Advik, you arrived halfway through my training, but you couldn't sense my pain. Amara, you came a year later and even you couldn't see how shattered I was. But Hritik, despite being a human, despite being a year younger than us, he understood me. He was never disgusted by me, never afraid. If anything, he loved me more because of my werewolf side, because he never lost sight of the person I was. He even kept my secret from his own sister. But he's gone now," Aisha sobbed, looking at Anjali. "Because of that daughter of yours who, despite your best efforts, will never belong here."

Amara gave her a pitying glance. "But *you* altered the full moon records, Aisha. You're equally responsible for Hritik's death."

"Don't you dare say his name," Aisha growled at her. "I didn't know why they made me ... I don't know why, it–"

"Oh, but I think you do," Aidan whispered.

"Regardless. They made you kill him," Amara said. "We would never."

Aisha hesitated. Genuine doubt played across her features. After a moment of contemplation, she glowered at Amara. "Nice try," she said, but her voice held a hint of uncertainty.

"So, you wanted to kill Kiara out of spite?" Anjali asked.

"Yes."

There was a long moment of silence.

"And is there a failsafe way to take out the Uprising for good?"

"No," Aisha said. "There is no failsafe way to take out the Uprising."

Anjali straightened in her chair. "Is there *any* way to destroy it?"

To Krish's surprise, Aisha grinned. "Of course, there is. It's not proven to be anything but a myth. The Elixir–and there's only one person here who can take it."

She turned to Kiara, and Krish's stomach dropped. Anjali's eyes widened. Amara's hand flew to her mouth.

"Oh God, no," Aidan breathed.

Advik and Kiara wore identical looks of confusion.

"We'll explain later," Amara said quickly to Kiara.

"I'm afraid I cannot allow my daughter and her companions to be present here any longer," Anjali said. "You are dismissed."

19

THE FIRST TIME Kiara had walked into the library, it had rendered her speechless. Stunning mahogany shelves lined the walls from top to bottom. Each shelf was divided into three or four cubicles. Each cubicle overflowed with books, separated by genre and alphabetized.

Now, a giant volume sat on the striking grey table at the centre of the room that held the coordinates for all the books in the library. Krish was flipping through it hurriedly.

"You don't need to look for it," Aidan said, sounding embarrassed. "I know where it is." He walked over and heaved a large book off a shelf on the far left. It was labelled *A Beginner's Guide to Katrols: Volume 1*. As he laid it down, Aidan gripped the table so tight it looked like he might break it.

Amara's eyes widened. She looked alarmed when she said, "Krish? Can we not use that one?"

"Why not?" he asked.

Amara chuckled nervously as she lifted the volume and passed it over to Aidan. "I mean, can't *we* just explain whatever is in there? Or draw it?"

"I'm sorry to have to break it to you, Mary," Advik said with a straight face. "But you can't draw to save your life. When you try to draw a flower, it looks like scribbles. If you try anything intricate, I'm afraid it'll look like, well, intricate scribbles."

"Why can't we use the book?" Kiara asked.

"It's nothing!" Amara said quickly.

"Okay then," Krish said, making to snatch the book from Aidan's grip, but he wouldn't let go. His smile was tight-lipped.

"What is wrong with you two?" Advik asked, grabbing the book.

Aidan made to take it back, but Kiara put her hand on his wrist. "I can handle it," she said.

Aidan shared a resigned glance with Amara. "All right," she conceded.

Krish took off the jacket and they all coughed as clouds of dust rose up into the air. Advik, overdramatic as ever, coughed significantly louder than the rest of them and clawed at his throat, making choking noises. He went on for far longer than the rest of them combined. Amara glared at him.

"Hey, man," Krish said, putting his hand on Advik's shoulder. "Is everything all right, you know, with your brain?"

Advik rolled his eyes. "All right, Krish. Let's hear your history lesson. Mary, not a word."

Krish looked like his birthday had been cancelled. He was horrible with names, and he was spectacularly abysmal at history. He took a deep breath; he wasn't about to back down from a challenge. "What was that guy's name again? A-gag-wuss?"

"A-goo-cuss?" Advik offered helpfully.

"Close enough," Amara said, failing to keep the amusement from her expression. "It's Agalecus."

"Thanks," Krish said. "And he had this–uh–this wife, called Silver-la–," he continued, but Amara cut him off.

"Advik, you've proven your point. Krish, I'm sorry, but you suck tremendously at this."

Advik grinned victoriously.

Amara flipped through the pages until she found one that read 'The Elixir'. She turned the book so they could all see the little drawings and illustrations. She pointed to certain pictures and started explaining. "This story is based in Ordenia itself. So Agalecus was a prodigy. At only nineteen years old, he was a master potioner. He could whip up just about anything. He was a genius, extremely good-looking and had a wealthy family. The only thing he lacked was physical strength, which he made up for with his charm and intelligence. There were a ridiculous number of suitors for him, but of course, he fell in love with the one person that didn't want him back. Her name was Sylvia."

"Wait, Mary," Advik said, his brow furrowed. He grunted as he tried to pry Amara's fingers away from the corner of the page, where there was an illustration of a small flame. "What's with the fire?"

"Oh, it's nothing."

"I want to know, too," Kiara said.

"Well, okay, then. Fire is a symbol associated with Katrols."

"Huh," Krish said. "Why?"

"I don't know."

"Amara ..." Krish prompted.

"I told you, I can take it," Kiara promised.

"Fine. Something to do with them wanting to burn the world down, or whatever, you know."

"Okay, that is *so* made up," Advik said. "You can't really think we'd believe that."

Amara shot him an accusatory glance, then shared one of deep understanding with Aidan.

"He's got a point, you know," Kiara said.

"Okay fine. There's a theory that Katrols possess a dark fire, which is the source of their powers."

"So, what? She's smoky Elsa now?" Advik asked.

"We don't actually know."

"What *do* we know for certain?" Kiara demanded.

"It's not exactly easy to pin down a Katrol for research, Kiara."

"Back to the matter at hand?" Advik intervened.

"Right, where was I?"

"Agalecus being an angsty, predictable teenager," Advik said.

"So, Agalecus whipped up the Elixir. It was supposed to imbue him with great physical power. He was also a Katrol, but didn't think that would change anything. Huge fault on his part."

Kiara shifted uncomfortably.

"Anyway, he brewed up the Elixir, the recipe of which he did not disclose to another living soul. Then he invited Sylvia for a moonlit walk on the beach, and took a swig of the Elixir in her presence. Sylvia watched, horrified and helpless, as he turned into a Katrol beast forever, ten times more vicious than the strongest Katrol. The next morning, her mother found her body on the beach, with what was remaining of the Elixir. Sapphire, Sylvia's mother, howled and mourned for her child for hours. She didn't know what the effects of the Elixir were, and vowed to find out the cause of her daughter's death and avenge her. So, she went to Agalecus's lab, and found a bubbling cauldron full of Elixir. She tested the potion on werewolves—Katrols and regular ones—and found that on regular werewolves, it worked just as it was designed to; it gave them an extra boost of strength. On Katrols though, it had one of two results: either the werewolf developed the strength and killing capacity of hundreds of human soldiers, or, if they weren't strong enough for the Elixir, they died. If the first one plays out, the werewolf remains a Katrol forever; they'll basically kill everyone in sight. Upon learning the horrifying effects of this particular brew, Sapphire was disgusted by it. Though she wanted revenge for her daughter, she knew that if she went hunting for the monster Agalecus had become, she wouldn't survive the encounter.

"So, she decided to honour her daughter's memory by keeping the world safe from the disastrous Elixir. She was unsure what the outcome would be if she simply discarded it, or whose hands it might fall into, or the destruction it could cause. She was a great believer in meditation and spirituality. So, she prayed and meditated for weeks after her daughter's death, and finally devoted the rest of her life to creating a series of obstacles that were extremely hard to cross to get to the Elixir.

"Despite her warnings, people who wanted to cause mass destruction attempted to get past these hurdles. It has been over two centuries since this took place. Over two centuries of people trying to obtain the Elixir for their own selfish reasons, thinking they could alter it to fit their needs. Till date, there have been no survivors."

"So, on that terrifyingly ominous note," Advik said, "what does all this have to do with Kiara?"

"Well, isn't it obvious?" Amara said sadly. "On the rest of us, it'll just act as a strength and energy booster. But if she drinks it, and it works correctly, we might have a chance at defeating the Katrols."

"So, I die anyway," Kiara concluded. "Even if I somehow pass all these insane obstacles and if the Elixir doesn't immediately kill me, I become a monster Katrol, slaughter the enemy and then you all will have to kill me."

Nobody argued.

"I'll do it. If that's what it takes to protect this place and the people in it, I'm ready to do it."

The room exploded.

"No!" Krish bellowed.

"Are you out of your damn mind?" Advik screamed, incredulous.

"How can you even think of doing something like that?" Aidan roared.

"Kiara, you can't do this to yourself," Amara said.

"That is not her decision to make," said an unfamiliar voice.

At the door of the library, stood a tall, pale man dressed in all black. He had a silver pin imitating the shape of a wolf on the collar of the long, black coat he wore over his suit. Even in the simple outfit, he looked regal and radiated power.

"President Silver," Krish breathed.

"Mr Oberoi. Ah, Kiara Sharma. It's a pleasure to make your acquaintance."

Kiara shook his outstretched hand, looking confused. "I'm sorry, do I know you?"

"No, Ms Sharma, I suppose you don't. I, on the other hand, know a great deal about you."

20

KIARA PULLED KRISH aside. "Wasn't Neil Raven the president?"

"Yeah, but he was poisoned three days ago, after the attack. No one knows who did it. It was an untraceable kill. The vice president chickened out. Nobody was willing to take the job. Silver was the only one who stepped up."

"Huh."

She opened her mouth to say more when the door flew open, revealing Anjali. "President Silver, what brings you here?" Anjali said, shaking his hand in a way that was strictly professional, but the tightness in her shoulders and her hardened jaw told Krish that Kiara's mother wasn't particularly fond of the president.

"Anjali," Silver said pleasantly. "Always a delight. Now, there's a very dire issue that I must discuss with you. I'm afraid it's about your daughter."

Subtle, Krish thought angrily.

Anjali's lips flattened into a thin line. "All right."

"We should go to your office. I'm not sure I'm comfortable discussing this in the presence of children," he said condescendingly.

"They're old enough," Anjali retorted in a steely voice. "Would you like a plush chair, or a throne, perhaps, to be comfortable?"

Silver chuckled. "Well, now, there's no need for that. If you're sure these children can handle it, just say the word and I'll begin."

"Please begin."

"All right then. You requested to harbour a Katrol here, and promised to tame her and train her, and you honestly exceeded my expectations. You managed to make her appear almost ordinary. Then I heard about the little incident that occurred recently. My deepest condolences," he added in the general direction of Kiara and her friends.

Kiara glared at him. Krish was impressed by her outright defiance.

"Now, I was completely taken aback," continued Silver, "because I had been extremely impressed by your progress. Mr Farber, the *cleaner*, has been telling me about everything that has happened here. Standard protocol suggests that Mr Oberoi, who failed his duty as a mentor, should be executed along with Ms Sharma for the crime."

A collective gasp rippled through the room.

"However, drastic times call for drastic measures," he continued after a long pause. "The Alphas and I tuned into Ms Waters's trial after hearing about the ... unfortunate incident. As punishment for their wrongdoings, your daughter and her mentor will need to go on a mission to find the Elixir. They can take their friends with them if they wish. I understand that Ms Sharma will not survive either way, but most werewolves prefer to go down fighting, am I right?"

Kiara looked like she agreed, but was stubbornly ignoring the president.

"A maximum of six kids leave in the morning exactly a week from now. I think the training they've had is the same as any adult here, and we need the adults to stay back here for work these children, however remarkable, cannot hope to accomplish. THIS–" he raised his voice, "–is not up for debate. It is the unanimous wish of the Alphas after careful deliberation. We're sorry it had to come to this, but these are express orders. Do you understand?"

"Yes, President Silver," Anjali and Krish echoed through gritted teeth.

"And you, Ms Sharma?"

"I got it," Kiara said in a clipped and sharp voice.

"I will give you some time to process this and discuss among yourselves. I have a few people I need to converse with."

As soon as the door clicked shut behind him, Anjali turned to her daughter. "I can help you and Krish escape, Kiara. Get away, settle somewhere else, start a new life. I'll–"

"No, Mumma. I'm doing this."

"Kiara–" Anjali protested sharply.

"You tried running away, Mumma. Twice. Because you thought it would help. But did it?"

"But–"

"Say I do what you're saying. Let's say Krish and I leave Ordenia. What difference will that make? I'll still be a Katrol. I'm beginning to realize I'm a liability either way. At least this way, I get to help the people I care about."

Anjali's expression hardened. "You don't have to do this. You know that, right?"

"But I do, Mumma. I really do."

She nodded.

"Well, obviously, I'm coming too," Aidan said.

"And me," Amara said.

Before anyone could protest, Advik said, "They're coming with you, and so am I, and there's nothing you can do about it."

Aidan slapped Advik on the back so hard that he winced slightly, but managed to pass it off as a cough. Amara smiled a little.

"Guys, this is on me and Kiara," Krish said. "There's absolutely no reason for you all to come."

"He's right," Kiara agreed. "We have no idea what's in store for us, and we can't allow you guys to risk your lives."

"You heard Advik," Amara said to Kiara. "There's no changing our minds now."

"But–"

"Nothing doing," Aidan said.

"Aidan, no," Krish said. "I know we've been through a lot together, but I can't let you sacrifice yourself for me."

"You both. This is about both of you."

"Aidan, you can't give up your life for a girl you've known for just a couple of weeks!" Kiara said.

"I'm going. And that's final," Aidan said stubbornly.

"But I can't let you do this for us–" Krish started.

"We are doing this for you, love," Amara said. "But we're also doing this for ourselves. For our Ordenia. This is our world, too."

Anjali put a weary hand on Kiara's shoulder. "I don't like you going any more than you like them going, but you have to let them make their own decisions."

Kiara changed the topic. "Where is this Elixir hidden, Mumma?"

Anjali retrieved a large map from a drawer in her desk. "I had Ms Aisha map out the layout of this–obstacle course?"

"Obstacle course is correct," Amara agreed.

"I had her swear that it is accurate. I assume you can navigate your way using a map. Once you enter the course, I'm so sorry, but you're on your own. We have very few records and information about what might await you. There could be creatures that you have never encountered, or worse, that you haven't even heard of, magic so potent that it cannot be fought, illusions that will make you think dark thoughts, unimaginable dangers–"

"All right, all right," Advik said. "We get the picture. It sounds like a really happy place."

"I'm sorry we can't do much to assist you. There is a lot to do and very little time to do it in. I could try negotiating with the president, but I'm afraid that will only make matters worse for you." She unrolled the map and laid it down on the table.

"It's easy enough to navigate," Anjali said. "It will be a three-day hike, and we will provide you with all the necessary resources, everything you need–"

"Wrong again, Anjali." President Silver was back.

"Pardon me?" Anjali said politely, but her tone said, "Really? This guy, again?"

"Yes, they are going on this mission for the good of Ordenia, but our resources are scarce and limited. I'm afraid we can only provide you with a small amount of help."

"Of course, president," Anjali said, barely controlled rage in her voice. "I understand our assets aren't exactly plentiful, but these children are going to do something rather vital for our survival. In fact, it could be exactly what we need for our survival. And they are very young. Surely, we can spare a little more–"

"No one regrets more than I that we cannot aid them further." He cleared his throat. "Now then, is it just going to be the sentenced?"

"These three have bravely volunteered," Anjali said, pointing at Amara, Aidan and Advik.

President Silver cast a disapproving glance at them. "And are you sure these, uh ... they will be capable of carrying out this operation?"

"I have absolute faith in them."

"Well, then, that's settled. Are my orders clear, Ms Sharma?"

"Crystal," she replied.

Most people would think that that was it. But Krish knew his best friend. Her eyebrows were slightly furrowed. She was biting her bottom lip and scowling slightly. She clearly could not stand him, and opened her mouth, perhaps to tell him just that, when her mother started speaking.

"President," Anjali said, "didn't you say that six was the limit?"

"Yes."

"I was thinking I could go with them. I might be able to guide them, and–"

"Let me stop you there, Anjali. You are indispensable for Ordenia in this hour of need. The five of them will go, and that is final. If you all can find someone to fill the sixth spot, you will need to have their name submitted to Anjali here within two days. I will return in a week's time to see our brave young wolves off. Good day to you."

He gave a polite smile, an impassive mask and walked out the door.

Krish felt Amara take his hand as the president's footsteps faded away.

Anjali was the first to regain her composure after a few minutes of silence. "Now, if you all will please pay attention to this map here," she continued. "You will need to venture back into the world of humans."

"Wait, what?" Amara said, surprised. "This astonishingly powerful magical object is just left out for the humans to snatch up?"

"I suggest you be patient and hear me out. In fact, I suggest all of you do the same," Anjali replied, not unkindly.

"You only explored Aarey Colony till our Ordenia. But beyond that, in the heart of the jungle, is where the obstacle course begins. It will take three days to reach your destination, but if you hurry, you could make it in two. I advise that you advance quickly, as the provided food and supplies will not be plenty. Do not overexert yourselves, though. That could be fatal."

The tension in the room increased noticeably.

"I expect that you all know how to use a map," Anjali said, looking expectantly at all the members of the group.

"Krish," she said, catching him off guard. She had never called him by his first name before. "I entrust you with the job of making sure this map is intact, at least until you no longer need it," she said, with a tiny hint of a smile.

"Now, Aidan, I think it is essential that you get all of them armed: with their own weapon, a gun with as many bullets as you can carry, a couple of tranquilizers and throwing stars and a blade. After this meeting concludes would be the best time to do it. I want both of you to take the rest of your team through stamina and strength-building exercises, supervised by one of our experts, starting first thing tomorrow morning."

"Okay, will do," Aidan replied.

"Advik, I want you to make a list of supplies that you feel you will need and report back to me by this evening, so I can try to secure as many of them as possible."

"Sounds good," Advik agreed.

"Amara, I need you to spend all your time at the library and research about anything and everything related to this matter. Knowing one simple fact could save your lives." Amara nodded silently.

Anjali turned to face her daughter. "Kiara, we will not be able to contact one another while you are on your mission. Your cell phones will not work in the forest, or in the obstacle course. You might encounter something that would be crucial for us to know back here in Ordenia, or we might discover some information that could help you inside the obstacle course, in which case we might need to get in touch with you."

Anjali brushed her hair back and unclasped the gold pendant that hung across her neck. It had a beautiful emerald, the size of a small marble. She put it in Kiara's palm. Kiara tried and failed to clasp the necklace around her throat.

"Need help?" Aidan offered.

Kiara smiled at him warmly. He gently brushed back her hair, and she blushed visibly. Aidan's own face looked flushed as he fastened the clasp and stepped back.

"Do you like it?" Anjali asked tentatively.

Kiara looked overcome at the vulnerability in her mother's voice. "I love it," she said in a surprisingly steady voice. "It's beautiful."

"It is," Anjali agreed. "But more importantly, it's magical. You have your friend to thank for that."

"Advik?" Kiara looked at him.

Advik blushed shyly. "I was just tinkering in the lab and mixing things around and ..."

"He's selling himself short," Anjali said. "He wasn't idly tinkering. He worked for days in that crummy lab trying to get this right."

"Well, what is it?"

"I have a ring with an identical stone on it. Advik created a potion so powerful that a simple coating of it on two similar surfaces enables users—wearers, in this case—to communicate long distance. So, while you're away, if you feel the need to share anything with me, or vice versa, we will be able to communicate through these. We can think of what we'd like to convey, say it out aloud or share Memory Orbs with one another."

"Advik, that's brilliant!" Kiara said.

"It was actually Aidan's idea," Advik said.

"Aidan?"

"Well, I thought there was a possibility that President Silver would banish you, so ..." Aidan trailed off, cheeks pink. "But, I mean, Advik is the one who actually did it. He should get all the credit."

"No, if you hadn't come up with the idea, I never would have—" Advik started.

"Thank you," Kiara said, her eyes shining with unshed tears, her voice small. The boys smiled.

"That will be all, then," Anjali said after a few beats. "Aidan, please arm them as soon as possible. And by all means, raid the kitchens if you need anything."

Advik smiled mischievously. *Uh oh*, Krish thought. *Bad idea.*

It was only when Advik yawned uproariously for the fourth time that Krish said, "Let's call it a night, shall we?"

It had been an eventful day. Following everything that had happened in the library, they had thrown themselves into preparations for their task. All five of them were armed to the teeth, their weapons stowed away carefully in their rooms. They created schedules and training timings and consulted their experts on any information they might need. They had taken an hour each with the experts to talk about survival skills, weapons, fighting techniques and basic medicine. Then they had all crashed in Kiara's room, utterly drained.

Getting up to leave, Amara kissed Kiara on the cheek.

"'Night," she muttered. Krish, too, nodded at Kiara on his way out, and Advik squeezed her shoulder as he left.

"Kiara ..." Aidan started.

"Don't say anything," Kiara whispered. "Please, I want to do this. I–I *need* to do this."

He took a seat beside her on the bed. "This is so beyond unfair. I'm really sorry."

She nodded mechanically. After a few moments of silence, she said, "Why did what Aisha say about Hugo trigger you so much? I know it wasn't something trivial. I saw it in your eyes, Aidan."

He sighed. "When I first Turned and entered Ordenia, Hugo was in charge, and Anjali was his apprentice. He was so driven, so passionate. He had this air of power about him. It was intoxicating. Looking back, it's probably why I was so infatuated with him in the first place."

"You were–?"

"I was in love with Hugo, yes." He added, "I like both men and women."

Kiara shrugged and smiled.

Aidan's brows furrowed in confusion. "What—no dramatic gasp?"

"Why would I do that? So you're bisexual. I don't see what the big deal is."

"I could kiss you right now," he breathed.

Kiara gazed into his eyes, her lips parted, heart hammering in her chest. *Kiss me.* Aidan's cheeks flushed at her reaction.

"Sorry ... it's just that my parents are less than progressive. They didn't handle my coming out so well."

Kiara's heart sank. She forced her face into a neutral expression so as to not betray her feelings.

"Anyway, this place was completely unrecognizable under Hugo's control. He was ambitious, yes, but with that came incessant brutality. He was brilliant, but violent and impatient. He also had this unfounded belief that anyone who disagreed with him—even about things that didn't matter—was not to be trusted. Despite my love for him, I didn't agree with his horribly violent agenda. So, one day, despite everything, I made the mistake of telling him that. He immediately had guards take me away. There was no truth serum at the time. Interrogations were done with a lie-detector of sorts. He plugged me in, and asked whether I was a spy, what my 'true motive' at Ordenia was. The machine proved to him that I wasn't lying.

"He was so angry about being wrong that he tore apart the machine. Bit by bit. Then he looked me in the eye and repeated all the same questions. I repeated what I had said earlier. He put his lips to my ear and whispered, 'I don't believe you.' I screamed and protested, but nothing I said stopped him from torturing me. He carved my back out, searing away my skin, ripping into my flesh."

Aidan turned his back to her and carefully pulled his shirt up and over his head. Kiara bit her lip to stop herself from screaming. This wasn't just any boy; this was Aidan. She knew she should have been rendered speechless.

But all she could see was what Hugo had done to Aidan's back. A gasp escaped her as she took it all in. She examined the pure distortion of his back, the warbled nature of the skin. Aidan hadn't been lying when he said that Hugo had quite literally carved through his flesh, cutting deep to his bones. She could see the places the knife had gashed his skin.

She looked at him and whispered, "May I?"

He nodded tightly, and shivered as Kiara ran her hand down his back, going over the bumps and planes, the warped lines and stitches that had sewn him back together. She traced his spine, fingers trembling. Aidan gasped slightly.

"I'm so sorry, Aidan."

"I was reporting for duty one day not too long after that," he continued, his voice now stripped of all composure. "And Anjali noticed that I was wincing every time I bent down. I–I told her that I was alright, but she insisted and took me to one of our healers. When Anjali saw my wounds, she was appalled and infuriated. She went around Ordenia to see if she could find any witnesses before she approached the Alphas to present my case. Everyone was too afraid to do it; they were too afraid of what he might do to them. Just as I had given up hope, three people volunteered: Advik, Krish and–"

"Amara?"

"Mary is just a few months older than you. She wasn't there at the time. She's January born."

"Well, nine months is hardly a few–it was Laura, wasn't it?"

Aidan nodded, eyes far off. "She was so ... you know those people who enter a room and everyone goes quiet to stare at them?"

Kiara thought back to the first time she'd seen Aidan. "I know the type."

"That was Laura. She was one of a kind; she lived in her own little bubble. And for whatever reason, I was lucky enough to be allowed inside."

Kiara knew she should feel a sharp stab of jealousy at the way Aidan talked about Laura. But how could she when she saw the grief on his face?

"Anyway, the Alphas replaced Hugo with Anjali, and he was exiled for a year, only to be let back in with a severe warning. There are a few people in Ordenia tasked with making sure he doesn't do anything like that ever again. Eyes are always following him."

Kiara nodded encouragingly at him. He continued, "Look, I know Aisha has done some horrible things. And I know the lie detecting procedure is much less painful now. But it just–it's hard for me to see someone go through that because I've been there. I know what it feels like. It's–" he broke off.

Kiara took his hand and squeezed it. He dropped his head on her shoulder. She knew nothing she could say would make it better. So, she just sat there in silence, Aidan's hand in hers, and let him have a moment away from the chaos of the world outside.

21

AMARA LAY ON her bed, twisting and turning. Now that Kiara knew about the fire within her, she had to warn her to help her. She climbed out of bed and pulled on a robe. She switched the lights on, blinking at the sudden brightness, and went to the door to open it. It didn't budge. She was sure it wasn't locked. Suddenly, she felt it twisting under her grip.

Someone was trying to open the door from the other side.

Amara's knife was on the shelf next to her bed. She would have to let go of the door in order to retrieve it. So, she held on to the knob and reached her free hand to the tiffin box on her study table. She managed to push the box off the table and flinched as it hit the floor with a thud, the impact forcing it open. She then grabbed the fork inside and held it tight as she let go of the knob, heartbeat racing.

The door swung open. Amara peeked around it and banged her head into someone else's. She shrieked and raised her fork when–

"Dammit, Mary!" Kiara shouted.

"Oh," Amara exclaimed, relief flooding in her. "Sorry."

Kiara was on the floor. Amara extended her arm and helped her up. They both massaged their foreheads and winced. Soon enough they were rolling on the floor, holding their stomachs and cracking up. Kiara wiped the tears from her eyes as Amara gasped for air.

Kiara cleared her throat. "Where were you off to?"

"To find you," Amara said. "I'm so sorry I told you about the fire like that, in front of everyone. It wasn't fair to you. I–"

"You don't owe me an apology. What you do owe me is an explanation."

"Right. The fire–have you encountered it before?"

Kiara bit her lip. "A few times."

"Oh my God!"

"What?"

"This fire, Kiara, it's bad–"

The doorknob rattled again, and the girls jumped as Aidan entered the room.

"Hey, Mary," he said. "About this fire–"

He stopped short as he saw the two of them on the floor.

"Kiara? What the hell are you doing here? And why are you guys on the floor?"

"The same as you, and it's a long story," Kiara answered.

"Okay, and ...?"

"And what?"

"What about this fire?"

"Apparently, it's bad."

Amara rolled her eyes. "It's the driving force for the Katrols. It's deadly and authoritative. It devours you whole when you Turn. You're blinded by this unreasonable yet compelling need to kill everything and everyone. And this fire, it gets worse as time wears on. Kiara, you asked why so much about your kind is uncertain. It's because a lot of Katrols let themselves get consumed by the fire, and it kills them."

"That's what's been happening," Aidan muttered to Kiara. She nodded.

Amara said, "What do you mean?"

"The day Kiara ... uh, the day we were in the library, she conjured up a ball of fire in her hand. And today, when we were at the trial, her hand burnt mine." He showed them the burn on his palm.

"That makes sense. The fire gets activated whenever an intense, negative emotion takes over," Amara said.

"How do we get rid of it?" Aidan asked.

"We can't."

Aidan shook his head. "There has to be something we can do."

"I think there is," Amara said, and Aidan perked up.

"Aisha said she's in the process of transforming from a Katrol to a regular wolf. That means the fire will be gone. And she knows how to put it out."

"But we have to leave–" Kiara started.

"We have six days."

Aidan put on a determined expression. "Let's go speak to an old friend, shall we?"

22

THERE WAS AN unspoken agreement between Kiara, Amara and Aidan to not disclose to the others what they were doing. They told Anjali they didn't want Hugo in the interrogation room this time, and that the CCTV cameras inside had to be switched off.

"Well, can you at least tell me what you're doing?" she asked. They shook their heads.

Anjali looked at Aidan. "Will this help my daughter?"

"We think so."

And that was it. Every day when the others were busy preparing for the insane journey awaiting them, Anjali would make up a story that required Aidan, Kiara and Amara to be near the interrogation room, and for the cameras to be switched off.

It was the day before they were scheduled to leave that a sense of urgency seized them. Their time was running out, and their patience was wearing thin.

"Aisha, for God's sake, stop that!" Aidan yelled. "What is wrong with you? Her life is at risk!"

The day was coming to an end and they still had no answers. Aisha was pretending to be asleep. They had resolved not to use any form of torture to get their answers, and since she had once been close to the three of them, she knew just how to get under their skin.

"Guys," Kiara said. "It's alright. I'm not going to survive much longer anyway. And besides, I have to be a Katrol when I take the Elixir. There's very little chance that you can take this fire out of me while I'm in wolf form. Thank you for trying. Thank you so much."

Amara slung an arm around her shoulder and started walking towards the door. Kiara turned back to face her old friend.

She looked at Aisha fondly. "I forgive you, Aish. Hritik never would have."

Aisha didn't respond, and the three of them walked out of the room.

But just before the door shut behind them, Kiara heard Aisha let out a sob and gasp, "No, he wouldn't have."

Krish was about to fall asleep when his watch started beeping. He looked at it, and his eyes widened in shock. Ordenia was being attacked again.

He ran out of the room with his backpack, and by the time he was in the corridor, Advik and Amara were by his side.

"Attack," Advik said.

"Yes," Amara confirmed.

"Guys, I need you to go to the kitchen and grab all the food and water you can stuff in our backpacks. The weaponry should have other basic equipment, tents, medicines. Grab anything and everything you can." He handed his backpack to Advik.

"What about you?" Advik asked.

"I'll get Aidan and Kiara. Meet in Anjali's office in ten?"

They nodded, looking determined, and took off at a run.

He reached Kiara's room and was about to throw the door open, when he heard two people conversing inside.

"This can't happen," Kiara was saying.

Krish pressed his ear against the door.

Kiara couldn't believe what she was hearing.

"Aidan," she said. "Are you really suggesting that we stay behind?"

"No," Aidan clarified. "I'm suggesting that we run away."

"Let me get this straight. You're suggesting we abandon our friends–and the whole of Ordenia–while they're literally out there fighting for their lives at this very moment?"

"That's not what I'm saying. I'm saying the whole group leaves for this obstacle course mission and instead of accompanying them, we lie low for a while and try to figure out some other way to solve this problem."

Kiara groaned in frustration. "Solve this, Aidan? We can't solve this! It's not a damn puzzle! It's people's lives that is being sacrificed out there, and their hopes are on us succeeding–on me succeeding."

"Kiara, I promise we'll figure something out to save these people, but you know you're not going to come out of this alive," Aidan yelled, and Kiara flinched. "What if you die before you even get your hands on the Elixir? Or worse, what if we go through the entire obstacle course and, against all odds, we get back to Ordenia with the Elixir, and your body rejects it, and you die anyway, leaving Ordenia none the safer, and leaving me without you!"

Kiara's eyes flew to his. "Aidan, I totally understand your logic. I see where you're coming from. But if I don't do this, it will eat me up inside. It's going to haunt me for the rest of my life that I had the power to put an end to this senseless war, and I refused to do anything about it. I know if the roles were reversed, I'd be having this argument with you, too. You're–" Kiara broke off.

How could she put into words how much he had come to mean to her in such a short period of time?

"You're one of my best friends," she decided. "Losing you would shatter me. And I'm sorry for what has to happen. I'm sorry that I'm going to leave you–that I *have* to leave you–but it's for your own good. It's for the good of Ordenia."

Aidan's control broke. "I'm one of your best friends, Kiara? Is that what you meant when you said you were 'a girl I'd only known for a couple of weeks'?"

Kiara stared at him evenly. "I appreciate the concern, but even Krish didn't try to talk me out of this. Why are you so adamant on not letting me go?"

"Because I'm terrified of losing you!" he screamed at last.

Kiara took his face in her hands and softly grazed his cheek with her thumb. "I'm sorry, but this has to happen. I have to do this."

He threw his hands in the air in exasperation.

"Kiara, you don't understand."

"What don't I understand?"

"You are–you're–you ..."

He broke off and kissed her.

One second, he was struggling to speak, and the next, his lips were on hers, passionate, desperate, as if trying to communicate what words couldn't. And then she was kissing him back, her mouth just as fervent on his soft lips. They moved against each other in a dance that was new and exciting, but also felt oddly familiar and inherently right. She ran her hands through his hair, and he wrapped his arms around her.

Aidan pulled away hesitantly. Suddenly, the need to touch him was overwhelming. Kiara closed the space between them once again, her arms going around his muscular frame, her lips on his. He held her roughly, hands caressing her in a way that caused tremors to spark through her body.

"Aidan," Kiara gasped as he led a trail of soft kisses up her neck. *Oh no*, she thought. *Aidan*. She broke the embrace abruptly and stepped away. His hair was dishevelled, and she could still feel the soft curls on her skin. His lips were pink and swollen from kissing, his face flushed to an alarming shade of pink.

"Kiara?" Aidan murmured, his eyes unfocused.

Kiara pressed her forehead to his. He closed his eyes and breathed softly against her neck. Her heart broke as she contemplated what she had to do next. Her mother's voice rang in her head: *Sometimes you have to break someone's heart for their own good.*

"Aidan," she said.

"Kiara," he responded, his voice full of longing. He *wanted* her.

"This can't happen." Kiara forced her voice not to break. "We can't happen."

Raw hurt and betrayal flashed in his eyes. She stepped slowly away from him.

"Because no matter what you tell yourself," she whispered, her voice shaking, "I am just a girl you've known for a few weeks. And I might not even be here in the next few. Forget me, Aidan."

Krish's heart ached for his best friend. He knew Kiara too well to not know what was going on inside her head: if Kiara broke Aidan's heart, he would hate her, and getting over her death would be that much easier.

Insensitive as it was, they had to leave now. He knocked roughly and pushed open the door. Kiara was on her bed, her head in her hands. Aidan's expression was one of agony. His hand lingered over his puffy lips.

Krish guessed what might have happened, but here was solid evidence.

"Everything okay in here?" Krish asked in an attempt to sound nonchalant.

"Fine!" they snapped in unison.

Krish lifted his arms in surrender.

"What's going on?" Kiara asked.

"There's been another attack. Gather your things, we have to go now."

Unsurprisingly, given that he'd been planning to run away with Kiara, Aidan had brought his own backpack to her room. They both strapped on their bags.

Kiara muttered to Aidan, "You still coming?"

Aidan nodded. "I want to spend as much time with you guys," he added as an afterthought, "as I can."

The three of them flew down multiple staircases and hallways, then raced into the main hall and doubled over, gasping for breath. Advik and Amara sprinted in, their backpacks bulging.

"We couldn't make it to the weaponry," Amara replied, panting.

"We got some sheets, hammers and nails for our shelter, but whatever weapons we have on us at the moment will have to do."

"What are we waiting for? Run, run, run!" Krish yelled.

They ran. They darted into Anjali's office without knocking, all manners and niceties forgotten.

"There you are!" she exclaimed. "You need to leave, now!" She reached over her head and yanked at a lever. A door in the wall at the back creaked open.

"This passageway leads to the edge of the forest. Go, go, go!"

They thanked her and bolted to the door. Krish stayed behind to hold the door open for the others. He saw Kiara hug her mother fiercely and blink back tears.

"I love you, Kie," Anjali was saying. "There's so much I wish I could tell you, but there isn't time. I'm so, so proud of you. And I can't even begin to imagine how much I'll miss you. You have turned out to be thrice the person I am, and I have no doubt you and your wonderfully talented friends will succeed in this mission."

Kiara blinked back tears. Krish had seen the relationship between the two women develop over the weeks. They had both been frustrated, angry and annoyed at each other. But in the end, their bond had prevailed. Kiara held on to her mother and cried openly. She clutched her mother like she never wanted to let go.

Anjali pulled away from Kiara, her eyes shining with tears, and tucked a lock of her daughter's hair behind her ear. Kiara closed her eyes and rested her head against her mother's hand.

Anjali said, in as steady a voice as she could, "Open your eyes, Kiara. Go."

Kiara nodded bravely and wiped her tears. She managed a watery smile.

"You okay?" Krish asked her, though he knew the answer.

"I'm fine. Let's go." She spared her mother one last glance. "Bye, Mumma!" she called and disappeared down the dark passageway.

Krish was on her heels. He let the door slam shut behind him with a resounding bang.

PART 3

23

"SHOULD WE STOP here?" Kiara asked. "Settle down for the night?" Kiara was only asking as a formality. It was obvious most of them had tired themselves out. Amara was ploughing ahead, the only one of them who wasn't half asleep. Advik had firmly planted his butt on the muddy ground and was refusing to move. Krish was chugging water from his bottle, half of it slopping down his shirt. Aidan's shirt and hair were soaked through with sweat. He licked his lips thirstily.

Earlier, they had kept up a steady pace as they entered the forest. They had walked a good half hour before they had been ambushed. People–who they could only assume were Katrols–had sprung out from behind the trees and lunged for them. Barely managing to hold them off, Kiara and the others had torn through the woods, the wind whooshing in their ears, thorns and leaves digging into their skin, roots attempting to trip them up at every turn.

And here they were two hours later: more trees and mud and trippy roots and howling winds.

"If you insist," Advik said in answer to Kiara's suggestion, trying to sound dignified. He failed miserably and slumped further into the mud.

"Honestly," Aidan said bravely, "I could walk for longer."

"All right," Amara said. "Let's go." She whirled around just in time to see him fall face-first onto the ground.

"As tired as we all are," Kiara said, "we can't be lax about security. There's five of us. We should keep watch in groups. We should manage at least four hours of sleep per person in two-hour shifts."

"Great idea, Kiara," Advik grumbled. "How about you and Aidan take the first shift?"

Aidan shrugged. "Sure."

"Actually," Amara piped up, her eyes reading the discomfort on Kiara's face, "you look exhausted, Aidan. You should get some rest. I'm awake. I'll take the shift with Kiara."

Kiara's sigh of relief was too prominent to mask. Aidan turned away. The two girls settled down on a fallen branch nearby while the others worked to set up the camp. Kiara expected Amara to ask about Aidan. But the other girl launched into discussion after discussion about trivial things.

"Aidan and I kissed," Kiara blurted out, interrupting her.

Amara nodded. Her expression was neutral. The surprise that Kiara expected to find was missing.

"What, you're not surprised?"

"I mean, I'm surprised he acted on his feelings and actually went for it, but if you're asking if I'm surprised that he has feelings for you—of course I'm not. Even a blind person could have seen the spark between you two. The way he looks at you ... it's like he has eyes only for you, like no matter how many people are present, you're the only one he sees, the only one he cares to see."

Kiara felt a lump in her throat. Amara changed the topic quickly. Two hours flew by as they talked about everything and nothing, cackling one moment, and close to tears the next.

As they talked, they felt the weight ease off their hearts. Then they sat in silence for a while, Kiara's head resting on Amara's shoulder, both plagued by the same thought: *how much more time do I have left with her?*

Soon enough, the camp was set, and everyone except the two of them had climbed into the makeshift tent. It would be a tight squeeze, but at least they'd be sheltered.

Advik and Aidan came over, marking the end of Kiara and Amara's shift.

"Krish looked too peaceful." Advik shrugged.

Kiara smiled fondly at the sleeping Krish as she crawled into their small sleeping spot. Hard as she tried, sleep wouldn't take her; her thoughts kept lingering on Aidan. A hollow pit carved its way into her stomach. She knew she couldn't be with him, that she had done what was best for him. She knew Aidan would eventually open his heart to someone else, once all this chaos had settled down, long after Kiara was dead and gone. Hot envy swept through her at the thought. She tossed and turned all night, unable to keep her mind from thoughts of a future that she could have had with Aidan.

Little did she know that he didn't sleep a wink that night either, believing she had easily drifted off to sleep.

A loud banging noise awoke Kiara. She instantly shot up, her hand reflexively reaching for Dawn. Dagger in hand, she scrambled out of the tent.

Advik had taken the liberty of being the alarm clock for the group. He clanged two pots together–the only utensils they'd been able to scavenge–and screamed at the top of his lungs.

Kiara was pleased to see he had cleaned himself up thoroughly and was dressed in a fresh set of clothes. Amara was glaring at Advik, and Krish simply refused to get out of bed.

Kiara allowed herself a quick look at Aidan. He was staring at her. They held each other's gaze for a moment. Kiara shivered; looking into his eyes still gave her butterflies. He broke away first, announcing that he was going to wash up in the nearby stream. Kiara forced herself to look away from him, eyes stinging as she did.

"All right, another successful day of walking," Aidan said that evening, his tone light and encouraging. "Now who's willing to take the first shift?"

Amara, just like the day before, was not tired. "I'm up."

"I'll take the shift with her," Krish ventured.

Amara's eyes lit up, her beautiful face breaking into a bright smile. While the others set up for the night, Krish strapped on his backpack and set off to explore their surroundings. He looked around at the lush trees with brightly coloured fruits.

I can make this work.

Twenty minutes later, he took Amara's hand and swiftly guided her to the small picnic he'd set up. It was far from ideal, but he had done the best he could, given the circumstances. But all his misgivings seemed to vanish as Amara leant over and kissed his cheek.

"I love it," she whispered.

Krish blushed. "Even the empty pans?"

"Especially the empty pans."

"They're not staying empty much longer. We're going berry picking."

"Berry picking–woah!" Amara giggled as Krish scooped her into his arms. She kicked off her shoes and wrapped her legs around his waist. He kissed her, a soft, sweet kiss.

Krish pulled away, grinning, and suddenly hoisted her up. She shrieked in delight as she reached up to a tree branch and plucked the first berry of the night.

They lost track of the time as the night progressed. Amara sat on Krish's shoulder, plucking berry after berry, throwing most of them into the pans and the others on Krish's head. Krish's shoulders shook as he laughed. Amara wobbled and slipped, laughing as he caught and embraced her. She leant her head against his chest. He held her tighter.

"You know," he whispered into her ear, "I think we got enough berries."

He set her down gently on the sheet he'd laid out and snuggled close to her. He was about to pop a berry into his mouth when Amara swatted his hand away.

"How do you know it's not poisonous?" she asked.

"Gut feeling," he said and, faster than she could stop him, popped the berry into his mouth.

Her jaw dropped in horror. He smiled.

"I'm kidding. I recognized these from my grandparents' farm in Rajasthan."

Amara punched his shoulder, hard.

"Hey!" he protested. "What was that for?"

She punched him again, harder. "The first one was for scaring the life out of me."

"And the second one?" She shrugged.

"Just felt like it."

Krish pulled her into his arms and kissed her hard. He knew there were things about that night that he would never forget: how she tasted of sweet berries, how perfectly their lips moved against each other's, how she slid her arms around his neck while their lips were locked, his hands finding their way into her hair.

They rolled on the grass, and Amara giggled, carefree and blissful. It was obvious she couldn't care less about the mud she was getting all over her clothes and in her hair.

They lay there for a while, gazing at the stars, hands clasping each other's tightly, hearts beating as one.

24

THE NEXT MORNING, the group started on their journey again, stopping at intervals to check the map that Anjali had given them. "Are we sure this whole saving Ordenia thing is really worth it?" Advik said peevishly.

"What do you mean?" Krish asked, bewildered.

"I mean, we could just come back another day, or leave it to someone else or–"

"Advik–"

"I know. The ragtag group of unqualified kids accomplishes what highly trained adults never could. But how are we supposed to get to the Elixir if–woah!"

Advik's knees gave out and he staggered, struggling to stay on his feet. Amara reached to help him, but followed suit.

Krish's eyebrows furrowed in confusion, but sure enough, in a matter of a few seconds, he felt it too. A gust of wind shoved him forward. It stabbed at his back painfully, forcing him to his knees. His vision grew blurry, dust blowing into his eyes. Arms flailing about wildly, he tried to grab on to anything to give him purchase. The wind grew louder, the noise deafening. He tried with all his might to get up, but the wind was too strong.

Krish struggled as his clothes stuck to his skin, pulling him in the opposite direction. His backpack seemed to suddenly be filled with rocks. He keeled over backwards, legs giving out completely. His arms were forced behind him. The thick, sturdy straps of his backpack were slowly slipping off. He was helpless to stop it from flying into the wind and disappearing into the abyss. He felt his weapons belt against his waist, blades cutting through his pants into his skin.

His mind went blank with panic as he called out, “Kiara! Kiara!”

He couldn’t hear his own voice. His throat felt raw and dry as dust entered his mouth. A violent cough racked through him, and his mouth was coated with the metallic taste of blood.

Aidan’s eyes were closing. His lungs were giving in. He couldn’t move, couldn’t breathe, couldn’t see.

“Shame,” he thought. “Really thought I’d live to see at least sixty.”

And just as his feet went out from under him, the unnatural wind stopped. Aidan managed to stay on his feet, surprising even himself. His palm was tightly clutching a smaller, more delicate one. He pried his eyes open to find Kiara staring back at him. He allowed himself a quick scan of her: her arms were all scratched and her eyes were red and twitching, but she looked okay otherwise. She was studying him carefully as well. She turned away hastily and withdrew her hand as his gaze met hers.

Aidan looked away to his other friends. They were inhaling fresh air like it was going out of stock. Krish’s pants were slit open, and blood oozed from his many wounds and cuts. Advik had welts all over his face. He was on the ground, legs crossed behind him. An unmoving Amara lay in front of him. He was periodically pumping her chest.

"Aidan!" Krish screamed.

Aidan ran. He dropped to his knees next to Advik and reached for the pouch strung on his hips. It was missing.

"Give her mouth-to-mouth!" he instructed Advik. Advik nodded and obeyed, then checked her pulse. His eyes must have shown his scepticism. Krish put his head in his hands. He gasped sharply and spat out blood.

"Kiara!" Aidan shouted. "Get my backpack!"

"Your backpack ... right. Where–where is it?"

"It must be here somewhere, I lost it in the wi–"

"No," Kiara breathed.

"What? Just get me the backpack, any backpack. They all have some basic medical equipment, I made sure of that."

"They're gone," Kiara said, panting. "All of them."

"That was the point of all this," Aidan said. "Ridding us of our supplies."

"What?" Kiara gasped. "We don't have anything else. Those backpacks were our only resources!"

Advik's face fell.

Kiara winced, staring at her palm. Aidan thought he saw something flickering there. Amara stirred. Krish let out a dry sob.

Amara coughed hoarsely. "Water," she rasped.

Krish looked around in a panic.

"We'll get her water," Advik whispered croakily. "She'll be okay."

"We don't know that, Advik!"

"I'm just trying to–"

"To what? Lighten the mood?"

"Guys–"

"Let's get her on her feet," Kiara suggested.

Together, she and Krish hoisted up a fragile Amara. Advik looked like he was struggling to get up, so Aidan offered him a hand. His heart lurched when he saw Advik limping.

He turned to Amara. "Mary," he said gently. "Can you walk?"

She nodded.

The earth exploded behind him.

The trees around them caught fire and collapsed over each other, the flames spreading rapidly. Waves of orange started making their way towards them. Aidan stared at the scene, transfixed in horror.

Krish finally came to his senses. "RUN!" he yelled.

Aidan saw Kiara sling one of Amara's arms over her shoulders, and Krish took the other. Aidan didn't need to be told twice. He spun on his heel, grabbed Advik's arm roughly, and sprinted.

They hadn't been running very long when they reached the edge of a cliff, below which was a seemingly calm water body. Aidan was about to jump, when a raspy voice rang in his ears.

Jump, it said, *and the fire jumps with you.*

The others, Aidan guessed, had also heard the voice. They all crowded around the edge of the cliff. He didn't need to turn around to see how close the flames were to them; he could feel the heat radiating off them.

In a last desperate attempt to save them, he yelled, "The voice has to be bluffing!"

"What if it's not?" Krish said fearfully.

"That's a chance we'll have to take!" Kiara screamed.

"I'd rather not be turned into a human marshmallow!" shrieked Advik.

"All right then!" Aidan bellowed. "On three!" He spared his friends one last glance, as if to say goodbye.

"One!" The fire was unnaturally close.

"Two!" He bent his knees to jump.

"Three!" He leapt.

25

KIARA HIT THE water hard. There was too much adrenaline in her veins to immediately feel the impact of the fall. Once she came up to the surface, she blinked the salty water out of her eyes and looked around desperately. Barely making out a blob of land in the distance, she frantically swam towards it and hauled herself up. She lay flat on her back, gasping for air and panting as she coughed up saltwater and waited for her friends to make their way there.

When the last of them had made it, a deep silence engulfed them, punctuated by the occasional hiccough or gasp.

"So, what now?" Advik asked tentatively.

Amara shrugged. "I guess we try to find a way off this place." Her voice still came out in rugged pants. Then she stepped back towards the shore and cupped some water in her palms. She brought the water to her mouth but shook her head, grimacing.

"As much as I'd like to get this over with," Kiara said, "we're in no condition to continue on right now. Let's just take a minute and breathe."

Krish nodded. "Is everyone okay?"

There was a chorus of scattered affirmations.

"Advik, buddy," Aidan said, "I hate to call you out, but your leg is not fine. In fact," he added, "I should probably check up on everyone. Krish, how much do you remember from the medical course we were all forced to take while preparing to be trainers?"

"Enough, I think."

Krish nodded at Aidan, and the two began to examine everyone in the group. Aidan went to Advik first. He knelt down beside his friend and gently pulled his pant leg up. Advik tried to bite back the wince that escaped him. Kiara's hand flew to her mouth in horror. Advik's leg was covered in *so much* blood. His pants were soaked through with it. Its metallic scent hung in the air ominously.

"Advikty Dumpty had a great fall?" Advik offered with a smile, but the pain in his eyes was unmistakeable. Aidan studied the wound carefully. He pulled out a small, white box from his weapons belt. Extracting a square of clean cloth from the box, he tenderly dabbed Advik's wound, telling him to breathe slowly through the sting.

Once the blood had been wiped away, Kiara could see the actual injury. She gagged. A long, deep gash made its way from Advik's knee all the way down to his toes. Aidan calmly assessed the wound, then retracted bandages and a tin container from his box. He pried the tin container open and rubbed some salve onto Advik's skin, murmuring soothingly. Kiara could almost hear Advik's flesh sizzle and sew itself back together. Advik blew out a sigh of relief. Aidan carefully bandaged the wound. He then stepped back to admire his handiwork, the sunlight sharpening his already chiselled face.

"That might leave a scar," Aidan informed Advik professionally.

Advik nodded serenely. "It's all part of the job." He caught Kiara's gaze and winked at her. She laughed weakly and returned the gesture. Krish fixed up Amara's forehead, and was now inspecting the wounds on his own abdomen.

"Well then," Aidan said, making his way over to Kiara. "I guess that leaves me with you."

Though her shoulder throbbed painfully, she hurriedly said, "I'm fine." She didn't feel she could handle being close to him now.

Aidan arched a brow. "No, you're not."

"Aidan, I told you, I'm alright."

"Kiara, I *know* that you're not," Aidan rebuffed. "Okay, I'll leave you alone."

"Thank God."

"On one condition."

"And that is ...?"

"Raise both your hands. High."

Kiara glared at him. He glared back. But his glare was softer, almost amused. He watched as Kiara slowly tried to make her hands go up. Her shoulder was killing her. God, she hated that he was right. She gritted her teeth so hard she was afraid he might hear them grind against each other. Kiara grimaced and lowered her arms. She cursed herself as Aidan's eyes narrowed in concern. He sat her down firmly.

"What?" Kiara demanded childishly. "I did what you asked."

"Oh, would you stop that?"

"Stop what?"

"This," he gestured at her, "this ridiculousness." His stare softened. "I know you're in pain, Kiara. Let me help you."

"Okay, fine."

She held her arm out reluctantly. She didn't think she imagined the relief on his face as he sat on his knees beside her. Kiara looked anywhere but at his face as he gently applied the salve and bandaged her up. His voice was slow, soft. The questions he asked, like 'is that all right' or 'does that hurt', made Kiara ache. He finished up with her, but lingered back. She found herself gaping at his mouth. She was so tired of resisting. Before she could catch ahold of herself, she was leaning in, her eyes fluttering close. She felt his palm cupping her face, exactly as it had a couple of days ago. But she'd stopped then, hadn't she? She'd thought he deserved to be with someone he could have a future with. And that hadn't changed.

Kiara's breath hitched and she drew back harshly. When she looked back at Aidan, he was already gone.

They spent the night on the island.

As a whole, the island was unimpressive to say the least. It was a large, mostly barren stretch of land with barely any grass and sparse trees. There was no one else around as far as they could tell. The trees themselves were unrecognizable to the lot of them, and they couldn't risk eating the deep purple pine-cone-shaped fruits.

It was the most uncomfortable night of Krish's life. He was sopping wet and cold. They didn't have spare clothes, or even a towel. They slept on the mud, teetering from the cold and starvation. Krish felt the urge to throw a temper tantrum. He finally fell into a restless sleep.

Krish's eyes cracked open at the break of dawn and went to his watch, but even that was broken. He sniffed the air. Was that smoke he smelt? He felt his mouth sour from morning breath. He splashed some water on his face to wake himself up, then realized he couldn't wipe it away. He shook his head rapidly, like the wet dog he felt like.

Then he shook his companions awake.

"So, what do we do now?" Advik asked.

"I guess we move forward," Kiara replied.

"There's another island, right there," Aidan observed, pointing at something that was so far away it looked like a mere speck. "But we can't exactly swim all the way, can we?"

"We have trees," Amara said.

"Advik has an axe," Krish remembered.

"I've seen my dad do this before," Kiara admitted.

"Well, then," Aidan said, his lips curving upward, "let's get building."

"Isn't she beautiful?" Aidan marvelled aloud, not for the first time.

"We managed to put something together, and it looks fine. Can we just go now?" Krish said.

Aidan glared at Krish.

"He's right," Advik said, looking amused.

Kiara, on the other hand, agreed with Aidan. She *was* beautiful. She had broken off a twig from a nearby tree and used it to sketch a rough instructional diagram, something she'd learned from her father the rare times she'd convinced him to take her along with him on his monthly 'fishing' trips with his college mates. (She doubted he'd caught more than five fish in all the years he'd been going.)

After hours of labour, more inane questions than Kiara could handle and a lot of frustrated arguing, they'd managed to build something of a boat. It was hugely flawed, with rickety sides and jagged edges, but they'd all squeezed in and sat there for several long minutes, to test its strength, and it had held up. Amara had sacrificed her many bracelets to fashion screws once they'd used up the ones Advik had had in his weapons belt. Kiara longed to run her brush over the boat's uneven wooden surface, and give it a personality, a story, but there was something so beautiful about a simple wooden boat that looked this imperfect.

They were all exhausted beyond measure by the time the last nail dug through the wood. They hadn't eaten all day, leaving them drained and famished. They unanimously agreed to just rip giant, chunky branches off trees to serve as oars, and even that took a lot more time than any of them would've liked.

Kiara could almost feel her arms grow heavier. Finally, they hopped onto the boat and folded in on themselves to try to take up as little space as possible. Even so, they were packed in like sardines. They rowed in peaceful quiet for a few long minutes ... or were they hours? Kiara could no longer tell how much time had passed, but the island barely looked any closer. They had three workable oars, and continued to pass them around every time one of them felt they couldn't continue any longer.

Suddenly a sharp ringing noise echoed in Kiara's ears. She drew in a breath and covered her ears with her hands. She felt Krish and Advik do the same next to her. She turned to Amara and screamed. That girl's eyes had become milky and unfocused. Her head had lolled to the side, and she was breathing eerily slowly.

"Aidan?" she heard Advik say, his voice strained.

Numb with fear, she looked to her friend to find him staring helplessly at Aidan, who was in the same reverie as Amara. Krish flailed his arms wildly in front of Amara's face, but she didn't even blink. Kiara slapped Aidan, but even then he didn't break out of his trance. The high-pitched noise grew louder, more intense. More painful. Kiara stifled a scream and stuffed her fingers into her ears.

Suddenly from the water around them, three figures emerged. They couldn't possibly be human, for they looked straight out of a fairytale, like mermaids. Long, pointed ears complemented large, round, forest-green eyes. Their full lips were almost unnaturally bright red. Cheekbones arched high on their faces, sculpting them into goddess-like works of art. Their skin was a gorgeous, almost metallic bronze. Gold coin-like tattoos glistened on their bodies, giving slight, tantalizing glimpses to the perfect figures that homed them. Their hair was the only thing that differentiated them. One had long, wavy dark blue hair, the colour of midnight skies. The second had short, bright green curls that matched her eyes perfectly. And the third, with straight hair the colour of fresh, blooming lavenders, had a gold tiara adorning her head. Their lips parted gracefully, musical notes thrumming out of them. Their screeches had morphed into hypnotizing music. As the boat grew nearer to these creatures, Kiara noticed other things: not only were their pupils green, but so were the rest of their eyes. Their hair ended in pointed tips, and was miraculously dry. Their tails glistened beneath the water. They had claws for hands, and their mouths were filled with pointed fangs coated in red.

Suddenly, their eyes turned black. Too late, Kiara caught on. Amara and Aidan rose in unison, leaning to jump into the water.

"We can't let them!" Kiara screamed, grabbing onto Amara's leg and pulling with all her might. "We can't let them get off the boat!"

Krish and Advik already had ahold of Aidan's torso and were trying to get him back in. But the two violently shook off their friends, their eyes locked on the mermaids in front of them. Kiara watched helplessly and in horror as they slid off their small boat and into the arms of the monstrous creatures. The mermaids smiled at Kiara and the boys as they pulled their friends into the water.

Kiara frantically dove into the water straightaway, and splashed around, but there was no trace of Aidan or Amara.

They were just gone.

26

AMARA FELT BLISS. Pure bliss. She was being dragged further into the depths of the water by a breathtaking beauty. Her hands gently tugged at hers. She had no idea how she could see so clearly underwater, but as long as she could see *her*, everything would be fine. She could vaguely make out Aidan's figure being escorted forward by the mermaid with midnight blue hair. Little pearls twinkled in it like stars. Aidan was looking at her like she was the only thing that mattered in the world, like she was the only thing he could see. Amara realized with a start that she had seen that look on Aidan's face before. Who did he look at like that? Her name was K ... Ki ...? She couldn't remember. Well, if she'd forgotten it, the girl couldn't have been too memorable.

Amara saw light reflecting on the dazzling tails of the mermaids in front of them. The mermaid accompanying her, and the one guiding Aidan, followed the third; their beautiful queen whose tiara glistened in the water. They moved in perfect synchronicity. They sparkled like diamonds in the water.

Krish watched slowly as the sunlight grew dimmer and dimmer, and he, Kiara and Advik plunged further into the dark depths of the merciless water. Advik was close to tears. They had scoured the waters around where their friends had vanished.

Well, scoured was putting it lightly. Short of literally tearing the sea apart, they had done everything they could.

Kiara had squealed excitedly when she saw something moving. She had captured it in her hand and brought it to the surface, only to yelp with horror and release the fish back into the water. Thankfully, it had survived.

Krish had let out a bark of triumph when he'd made contact with a particularly smooth, light rock. It'd turned quickly into a moan of dejection as he discovered its true nature.

"Anything?" Advik called to the others.

"No!" Kiara yelled back.

"I got nothing!" Krish said in response.

It was true. They really had nothing.

Kiara thought she had experienced hopelessness before, but it was nothing compared to the pure despair she felt at the moment. She wanted to curl up into a little ball and sob, till she had no more tears left, about everything that had happened since she'd Turned. Instead, she decided to broach the inevitable question with the boys.

Advik had his sweatpants rolled up to his knees. He was bent over the water, eyes scanning its depths for any sign of their friends. Krish was completely immersed in the very shallow water, arms scrambling for any sign of life. There were cuts all along his arms, little red gashes where he'd scraped them against the stones.

"Guys," she said, "I think we have to go on."

"Without the others?" Advik asked, perplexed.

"Yes, we have to." Krish's voice was steely and mechanical.

Advik stared at them with wide eyes, looking horrified.

Kiara pushed the hair out of her eyes. Her fingers had become wrinkled from the prolonged contact with salty water. Resigned, she swam back to the boat, wishing a mermaid would emerge and take her into the unforgiving water, and wasn't even out of breath when she climbed back in.

Advik and Krish were already seated on the wood, waiting for her. Krish's stomach grumbled. He reached into his weapons belt and produced an entire bar of chocolate. He tore open the wrapper and divided the chocolate into three equal pieces, handing one each to Kiara and Advik.

"Eat," he commanded, and they didn't hesitate.

"How ...?" Kiara murmured as she dug her teeth into the bar, almost ferociously. "Why didn't you mention that you had food earlier?"

"Anjali says that you should always have some kind of energy-inducing snack on you, especially while fighting. Plus, you don't get through a medical course without knowing to always carry food. Starvation is a really long, drawn-out way to die. And I was kind of saving it for when things got really bad," he explained, and added, "which they are now."

Kiara swallowed, hard. She tried to concentrate solely on the chocolate in her mouth. She tipped her head back and moaned contentedly. Out of the corner of her eye, she watched Krish's failed attempt to mask the fond smile that crept up his face. Sighing contentedly when she finished eating, she nodded at the others, and they started making their way across the water again.

Kiara shivered as a cold breeze pushed the boat ahead towards the island. It was right in front of them now. She raised her hand to touch the land, to haul herself up onto it, but found that she couldn't. It was like there was some invisible barrier preventing her from making contact.

She tried over and over again, but every time her hand met the barrier. She kicked and flailed her arms around, to no effect.

At last, she rasped out, "I don't think we can go unless we have the entire ensemble."

Krish's eyes glossed over with relieved tears. "Sorry," he said guiltily, his voice quivering, "I didn't want to continue without them."

Kiara didn't *want* to continue without them either. Her frustration caused sparks in her fingers. She shook them hurriedly and dunked them underwater. The flame remained untouched.

What were they going to do now?

Aidan wasn't sure how long he could hold his breath underwater before his lungs gave out.

He made a slight gurgling noise. His mermaid turned towards him and smiled. Her eyes, the colour of seaweed, lit up brightly. Her hair cascaded behind her like a dark map of the sky, glittering with pearls. Her lips were ...

Her lips are all right, Aidan thought. He'd seen better lips elsewhere. He couldn't remember where exactly. But he just knew he had. He snapped out of his trance and let out a hoard of bubbles from his mouth.

He remembered. He remembered her.

Kiara.

Just then, the mermaid turned her face to his and grabbed him by the collar. He struggled against her for a short moment as she wrapped her arms around his neck and kissed him on the mouth. All consciousness leaked away from him as he immersed himself into her. He was so entranced that he didn't realize he tasted blood. His own blood. She was using her sharp, almost fang-like teeth to cut into his lips.

He opened his eyes to find his vision blurred with red.

"Guys!" Advik yelled. "Look!"

Krish turned over to the edge of the boat where Advik was sitting. He knelt beside him and grabbed his wrist. When Advik spoke, his eyes were desperate. Desperate and terrified.

"What is it?" Kiara asked.

"Don't you see that?"

"See what?"

"Red bubbles! There!"

Kiara's control snapped. "Advik, are you serious? I get that you're tired and probably just trying to lighten the mood by cracking one of your jokes that I really don't get, but guess what? This is not the damn time for jokes! My friends could be dying down there, so grow the hell up!"

"Kiara?" Krish whispered, shocked.

"Stop," Advik said. "They're my friends too, Kiara. I would never do something that cruel. And I swear," he added shakily, "I really did see bubbles."

Kiara felt a pang of regret. She was so caught up in her anger, in her bitterness, that she'd taken it out on the person who deserved it the least. "Advik, I–" Her voice broke, and she just looked at him. He nodded resignedly. More rage flooded through Kiara's body: at herself this time, for making her friend look so miserable. Fire sparked on her fingertips. She tried to blow it out irritably. Suddenly, her eyes widened in shock.

"I've got it," she breathed. "I–I've got it."

Krish's head turned in her direction. "What do you mean?"

She raised her hand. Advik flinched in surprise and fear. Krish's eyebrows shot up.

"This flame doesn't get doused by water. What if I can use it to manipulate the water?" she said, almost excitedly.

"I don't know if it will work, Kiara," Krish said.

Kiara's spirit deflated a little.

"But it's all we've got. I say give it a shot."

"Advik, where did you see the bubbles?"

He pointed at a spot to her right.

Kiara urged the flames to grow. She ordered them. Her eyelids fluttered shut as she reached inside herself, into her very being, and pulled the fire out. She rocked back slightly as flames shot out of her palms. Their colour was everchanging; purple one second, blue the next.

She pushed her hands further towards the water. Her hair blew back, her eyes flashed open. She looked at the fire before her, the fire that was a part of Kiara. A part that she had kept under cover for the longest time, and was now ready to display proudly. Her eyes turned a blinding red, all traces of their previous brown erased.

The waves remained still. Unmoving.

Hot tears of anger and disappointment flowed down her cheeks but she wiped them away hastily. She turned around to climb back onto the boat, and bumped into Advik.

She looked up at him and fell against him as his arms went around her. "I'm sorry," she said, her voice muffled. "I don't know what I'm doing and I'm so lost, and you didn't deserve that, and God, I'm so sorry."

"Shh," he whispered into her hair. She took a deep breath and started pulling away when–

"Ouch."

Advik's nail had accidentally grazed her arm, and a small cut appeared. A few drops of blood oozed out of it.

Kiara winced. "I'll just wash it, it's no big deal," she said to an apologetic Advik. She lowered the stinging cut into the water. She heard a slight gurgling sound from the water, and suddenly, her arm stung maddeningly. Blood was now gushing out of the cut at an alarming rate. Kiara screamed and tried to pull her arm out, but it wouldn't budge. She hissed in pain as the two boys tried heaving her out of the water.

As the three of them watched in shock, the water split open. In the chasm, Kiara watched in shock as the waves broke apart, and made way where her blood poured. She could see people.

They saw the mermaids with their friends. Aidan was unconscious in one's arms, his lips red. Amara had gashes along her collarbones and her clothes were torn and patchy.

But when she took a whiff of the clean, fresh air, Amara seemed to snap out of her reverie, while Aidan remained unmoving. Kiara could see Krish's shoulders sag in relief. He threw a well-aimed throwing star at Amara's captor's throat, and she screeched and fell back into the water.

Kiara hitched a painful breath as Advik ran to her. He grabbed her shoulders and lifted her above the water. The third mermaid had sunk her fangs into Kiara's wound and was draining it aggressively. Advik hastily grabbed a dagger and sliced her head off in a clean arc. The seafoam bubbled as it took her back.

Kiara shook compulsively, her body weakened from the heavy blood loss. Advik made to steady her, but she rasped, "One last thing."

The only word Krish could use to describe Kiara's expression, even vaguely, was thunderous. The mermaid holding Aidan threw him aside as she saw Kiara approaching. Krish almost flew across the water to catch him. The mermaid growled at Kiara and snapped her claws threateningly, ready to strike. Although the mermaid looked deadly, the look in Kiara's eyes said she'd already won.

Before the mermaid could even move, Kiara stabbed her viciously in the eye. Krish hadn't even seen her unsheathe her dagger. She howled in pain as Kiara extracted the blade from her eye, and shoved it into her stomach. The sea creature let out a blood-curdling yelp; her eyes rolled back and she exploded into a shower of dust, joining her companions in the water.

They all stared at each other for a long time, in disbelief of what had just happened. Amara was the first to come to her senses. Panting, she said, "The other island."

They waded across the water lousily, Advik supporting Amara and Kiara, and Krish half-carrying Aidan. Once they all painstakingly made it near the shore, they pressed one palm each onto the invisible barrier. Krish held Aidan's hand to it.

It broke.

They scrambled onto the stretch of land. Krish lay Aidan down gently. Kiara immediately knelt beside him, but looked like she was going to pass out any second herself. Tears glistened in her eyes. She pushed Aidan's hair back affectionately.

"Wake up, Aidan," she whispered. "Please, wake up."

He stirred. Krish bit back a howl of relief.

"Kiara," Aidan said, barely audibly. The second he opened his eyes, he cupped her face with his palm. She hastily wiped the tears from her eyes. The raw, vulnerable expression she wore mere seconds ago was gone, replaced by a hard, blank mask. She stood up, and his hand thudded back to the ground.

Hurt flashed across Aidan's face, but Kiara didn't look back to see it. Instead, she sat next to Advik. "Advik, I–"

He held up his hand. "You're a Katrol. You're acting like one. I get it."

"And that's the problem."

"What do you mean? You're just behaving like a Katrol, are you not?"

"No, Advik. I am sorry. I don't want you to 'get it'. I shouldn't have screamed at you. That was uncalled for. I can't keep using who I am–what I am–as an excuse for my actions. I have to take responsibility for them, Katrol or not. So, for whatever I've done and said to hurt you, I'm truly sorry. I know you're doing all this for me, risking your life for me. Thank you."

Advik swallowed and nodded, a small smile pulling at the corners of his mouth.

"So, uh," Amara said. "We're back."

There was a flurry of relieved hugs. Aidan seemed to have recovered, but didn't join them.

Soon they found themselves sitting in a small circle, making light conversation, even surprising themselves by laughing occasionally. Krish and Amara sat huddled together as he fussed over the fresh cuts on her body. Aidan recounted his experience underwater to a fascinated Advik.

"Amara?" Kiara said, nudging her. "Aidan? I need to talk to you guys for a second." Amara saw that her eyes glittered with tears.

Aidan raised his eyebrows. "Sure."

"The fire, Mary," she whispered once they were out of earshot of the others. "I feel little jolts of it before I go to sleep. I woke up today with some grass around me, aflame. And since the river incident it hasn't gone out at all. Don't get me wrong, I'd do it a thousand times over if there was even the slightest chance of it working. But I'm worried. You both researched Katrols for a while. Is there anything that can be done?"

Amara reached out to squeeze Kiara's hand, but she recoiled.

"Don't," she said. "I'm sorry."

She turned to Aidan, who shook his head as well.

Kiara smiled, an unbearably sad and resigned smile that broke Amara's heart. "Thanks anyway."

They walked back and rejoined the group. Krish opened his mouth, probably to ask what they were discussing, when he was loudly interrupted. The ground itself rumbled and shook violently, and a crack appeared before them.

Screaming, Amara turned to jump off the island, into the water, only to find that it had seemingly winked out of existence.

They were now on a solid mass of land. An *unending* mass of land. The boat they'd spent long hours making lay broken on the side.

Advik yelped as the crack in the earth got wider. The group unintentionally divided themselves into two. Amara, Advik and Kiara leapt onto one side while Krish and Aidan bolted to the other. The ground roared. Amara teetered on the edge of the abyss. She tried to regain her balance. After a few seconds of struggle, she managed to stand.

She let out a scream as her legs tangled up with a branch and she fell backwards into the gaping mouth of the crack.

27

KIARA COULDN'T SEE anything.

The ground was shaking so severely that her legs gave out. She was flat on her back when she heard Amara yell. Krish called out her name. Kiara couldn't feel the earth beneath her anymore.

Somehow, her legs held her weight. She ran across to where Amara had been standing, not caring that there was a chance of her falling off, and threw herself to the ground. She panted as she dangled off the crack's edge to catch her friend's hand. Her fingers tightened around it.

"I–got–you," she gasped. Her hands grew slick with sweat. "Help me help you, you're slipping away!" Amara's grip hardened.

Kiara could feel the other girl straining and pulling herself up. Kiara yanked on her hand, and finally hauled her back on land. Everything stopped moving. Kiara and Amara lay still on the grass. Amara got up and pulled Kiara up with her.

"Thank you," she whispered, tears streaking her face.

"Of course," Kiara replied.

"Kiara. Amara." Advik looked panicked.

"We're okay," Kiara reassured him.

"Now what?" Amara said, still shaking.

"I guess we move forward." Amara turned to Krish on the other side of the divide and yelled. "Cross over to the other side! We have to continue."

Kiara could tell she was trying very hard to keep her voice steady.

"Figure something out. But please survive, for me! We'll meet again, I promise."

A look of raw vulnerability flashed across Krish's face, but all he did was nod.

Kiara glanced at Aidan to see his eyes on her. "You got this," he mouthed. And for the first time in what felt like ages, she smiled at him.

Aidan trudged through the grass grumpily.

"So let me get this straight," Krish said, not for the first time. "We're supposed to build an entire bridge to go across?"

Aidan's jaw hardened. "Yes," he said wearily.

"You Turned before me," Krish said. "Tell me you have some magic werewolf thingy to get us out of this situation."

"I have a magic werewolf thingy to get us out of this situation," Aidan echoed loyally.

"Well, do you?"

"I do not. I guess we better get building," Aidan said.

"Listen, our training in building only covered so much. A boat is one thing. But a whole bridge? Isn't that a little too far-fetched?"

"It is. We can't just build a bridge." Aidan walked over to the edge of the crack. "It's not too wide. I bet we could jump across."

"Jump?" Krish scoffed. "Absolutely not."

"What do you think the others are doing?" Aidan ventured after a while, clearly struggling to strike up a conversation.

"I think they're fighting off ... a pride of lions!" Krish ventured.

Aidan arched his brows. "Lions?" His voice was drowning in sarcasm.

"Hey, it could happen."

"I'd like to see *you* battling some lions."

"I could, you know, I–"

"I bet," Aidan screamed over the other boy, "that they're already back in Ordenia and have found a way to end everything without Kiara dying, and they'll live happily ever after while we sit here trying to decide whether or not to jump for the rest of our lives."

"You are *so* not jumping."

"But–"

"No, there's no but here, okay? You're not jumping."

"Why?"

"Because–"

"Because I'm your friend? Come on, Krish, we've done so many reckless things together. What's changed?"

"Kiara!" Krish said, exasperated.

"What about her?"

"Well, in case you haven't noticed, my best friend has fallen head over heels for you. So yes, you're my friend. And yes, we've done crazier things in the last two years. But I have to keep you safe now. For her."

Aidan closed his eyes and swallowed hard. For a few moments, neither of them said anything. Krish's heavy, angry breathing calmed.

"I have," Aidan whispered, almost inaudibly.

"You have what?"

"I have noticed."

Krish nodded. There was so much more Aidan could've said, but he felt he didn't need to. Krish understood.

"Rope. Is there any way we can fashion one?" Krish said.

"Now there's an idea."

They spent the day scouting the stretch of land they were stranded on, and found a tangle of vines and weeds to begin sawing off slowly. Small welts bloomed on their hands and arms as hours flew by. When the night fell, blanketing them in darkness, they decided to continue the next morning.

Aidan crashed onto the rough grass and let the darkness claim him.

How long had it been? It had to have been a good few hours. At *least* a good few hours. There was no way to truly know. The sun sweltered on, looking the same as it had a lifetime ago, when the crack had first formed. The crack which was now out of sight.

Amara almost fell to her knees from exhaustion. Her eyes watered, perspiration drenched her back and her legs felt like jelly.

"Hey, Mary?" Advik asked. "You good?"

Kiara eyed her. "Let's call it a day, get some rest."

Amara shot her a grateful glance.

"Crazy, isn't it? All that we have already been through ..." Advik ventured. "We travelled on foot through an insane semi-tornado situation, then you guys were taken hostage by crazy hot mermaids–"

"Advik!"

"What? I'm not saying I liked them, but I'm also not saying I *dis*liked looking at them. And then the bloody ground split open. I mean, what could we have possibly done to offend all the elements?"

Amara felt a pang at the truth behind his jokes. First the wind, then the water and then the earth had acted against them. Her eyes suddenly widened as realization hit her. She ran over to Advik and planted a peck on his cheek.

He smiled at her. "What was that for?"

"Advik, you genius."

"I *am* smart," he agreed. "But ... why, exactly?"

"You just said it–we seem to have triggered *all the elements*."

Kiara's hand flew to her mouth. "The elements! Air, water, earth, fire and in some cases, the human spirit."

Amara nodded excitedly.

"So hypothetically," Advik said, "if that's true, we're only left with two obstacles at most."

"Maybe we should let Anjali know."

"I don't exactly know how this works," Kiara said, pointing to her necklace. She tentatively opened the locket and pressed her lips to its cold, steely surface.

"Mumma?" she whispered. "Are you there?"

"Kiara," her mother's voice answered. "Is everything all right?"

She sounded scared and exhausted. Moisture built in Kiara's eyes. Amara could see her stubbornly trying to hold back her tears.

"Mumma," she said, her voice fragile. "Are you alright? You sound–"

"Of course, I'm alright," Anjali snapped, a little too harshly for it to be the truth.

Kiara expelled an annoyed breath. "How's everything at Ordenia?"

Amara heard Anjali draw in a sharp breath. "Would you like the real or the sugar-coated answer?"

"Never mind," Kiara muttered. "I just wanted to let you know we're more than halfway through with the obstacles, and we have a good grip on what we're going to encounter."

Amara could almost hear the strained smile in Anjali's voice. "That's great, love. Please make haste, but don't be careless."

"I won't. I promise."

"Good girl."

"How long has it been since we left?"

"Two weeks."

Amara's heart stuttered. *Two weeks?* The amount of damage that could've happened at Ordenia in that time ... She shuddered and refused to think about it.

Kiara seemed to be thinking around the same lines. "I'll see you, Mumma."

"I love you, Kiara."

Kiara snapped her necklace shut and swallowed hard. Advik put a comforting hand on her shoulder. Her stomach growled in response. Advik scowled at it. "Hey, I was just trying to be nice." Kiara cracked a weak smile.

"But, in all seriousness," he added, "we'll starve to death if we don't find something to eat, and soon."

"There's always the weird-looking fruits on the trees," Kiara suggested.

"But we can't know that they aren't poisonous."

"I guess," Kiara said, running towards the trees and calling over her shoulder, "that's a chance we'll have to take."

Amara put her palm to her forehead. What was with all the recklessness? "Maybe we should take a second to think," she said.

"I did think of something," Kiara said, her arms bursting with colourful, juicy-looking fruits. "I know I'm not going to make it once I have a sip of the Elixir, and I might not make it past this–whatever it is."

She reached behind her neck to unclasp the necklace, and shivered. Advik raised a puzzled brow, but Amara was aware why Kiara looked so pained as she made to loop the chain around Amara's neck. Amara remembered how lovingly Aidan had made Kiara wear it, the look in his eyes as he'd gazed at her, the sharp intake of breath he'd expelled when his fingers had brushed her neck. Amara swatted her hand away, none too gently.

"No."

Kiara looked hurt and disoriented. "No?"

"That is your mother's locket. Her gift to you. You should've seen the joy on her face when she saw it bouncing around your neck. The pride. The love. So, I don't care what happens, no one is going to take that away from you."

Amara reached out and clasped the locket back around Kiara's neck. Advik exhaled deeply.

"Kiara," Advik said, turning to her. "I'm just here doing all this to make sure you succeed. To make sure that Ordenia is safe. It is possible that Amara's right. The fruits could be dangerous, poisonous, maybe even lethal. I–I can taste them first, and you'll be safe."

Kiara's expression softened. "Advik, that's incredibly sweet. But as famished as I am, it's just food. We've lived without it so far, what's a little longer?"

Kiara threw the pieces of the fruit she'd cut with Dawn, and made to sheathe the blade. She sucked on her thumb. She looked like she was on the verge of collapsing.

"Let me take care of that," Amara offered. She took Dawn and put it back in Kiara's belt.

And suddenly, everything happened at once: the earth exploded, literally, and sent Amara and her companions flying back. She hit the ground with such force she could swear she heard her collarbone crack as smoke clouded her vision. An agonizing cry tore free from her throat and she heard a similar one to her right: a male voice this time. She swallowed the lump in her throat and prayed to the heavens that Advik was uninjured. Something sprouted beside her. She squirmed away.

Was it ... a plant? What was happening?

Her throat closed up when she opened her mouth to call out to her friends, dust flying into it, causing a violent coughing fit. Her eyelashes batted furiously in an attempt to keep her eyes open. But they grew blurry with tears; she couldn't see anything.

The last thing she saw was flowers and leaves drifting past her in a swift and coordinated dance, as if alive, before she finally succumbed to the darkness.

28

AIDAN WOKE UP to find himself covered in leaves.

He yelped and sprung up, only to see Krish's laughing face. "Very funny," he said dryly. "Ha ha." He rubbed his eyes groggily and groaned. "You know what I really want? I want to wake up in my bed in Ordenia and realize this was all just a horrible nightmare."

Krish looked at him sadly, all humour gone. "Me too."

"So, we have a bit of a problem," Krish continued, scratching his head.

"A bit of a problem?" Aidan said, still struggling to wrap his head around the situation.

"We don't have any way to contact the others, no way to know if there's more danger there or if they need us to stay here for a bit."

"That's something we'll just have to risk, I guess."

"Yeah, well," Krish sighed. "I woke up a while ago, and–" He pointed to a heap of stringy vines on his right.

"You managed all that?" Aidan could've kissed him.

Unprompted and unwanted, a memory crept up on him. "I could kiss you right now," he'd told Kiara. Her mouth had opened in what Aidan could only assume was horror. A traitorous blush had snuck up on his cheeks.

But he *had* kissed her. He had kissed and held her, for an overwhelming and all-consuming few moments, dominated by the feeling of her lips, her touch, the feeling of her pressed up against him–

Krish waved a hand in front of his face. "Earth to Aidan."

Aidan scowled, embarrassed. "Sorry."

"Is everything okay?" Krish asked.

"I'm good."

"In that case, let's get to work."

As it turned out, work was not fun. Not only did they have to cut the vines carefully, but they also had to search for more clumps of them. Not to mention the part that came afterwards, to actually figure out a way to weave them together and make that clump strong enough to hold their body weight. Soon Krish was doubled over, panting. Aidan wiped at the perspiration building up on his forehead, but kept going.

"What are you made of?" Krish asked him in awe.

"Determination? Desperation? I can't tell."

Krish tipped an imaginary hat in respect and hauled himself back up.

Aidan's mood worsened as the night crept across the sky once again. They'd barely made any progress. He wondered what Advik and Amara were up to. He wondered what Kiara was up to.

Wherever you are, Kiara, he thought, *whatever you're doing, just hold on a little longer. We're coming to get you.*

Just hold on.

Kiara held on for dear life as the earth shook.

Her eyes shuttered open and shut over and over again, drinking in as much light as they could. She was pushed back as a massive wave of wind threatened to take her under.

She wrapped her arms desperately around a massive tree trunk, dangling uselessly from it. Her arms trembled against the force of the wind. She closed her eyes as they gave way and she nearly flew off with the wind. Then, the wind stopped just as abruptly as it had started.

She thudded to the ground and clutched her elbow, which throbbed painfully. Her fingers came away red. She bit back a scream and tasted fresh blood. She forced herself to get up, even though her entire body ached badly, even though getting up was the last thing she wanted to do. She snorted. None of this was what she'd wanted to do.

She was sure she was delirious when she noticed plants moving rhythmically in the fuzzy air. It was like the leaves, roots, fruits, branches and flowers had come alive. They frolicked and pranced in a measured, almost practiced waltz. They arranged themselves artfully in front of her eyes. Then the fog cleared and she saw the still bodies of her two friends.

Kiara let loose a screech of horror and she raced to inspect Advik. The flesh on his forehead was torn open, and his face was painted with gore. It seemed like the wound on his leg had reopened, and a large chunk from the bottom of his jeans was missing, exposing the gashes on his leg.

Kiara whimpered weakly as tears threatened to come to her eyes.

"Aidan?" she called out. "Krish?" But of course, the two people, the only two people who could have helped her out right now, were not present. She squeezed Advik's hand and felt her tears mingle with the red on it. His pulse was slight, but it was there.

She made her way slowly, defeatedly, towards Amara's body, and unconsciously wrinkled her nose at the puddle of sick her friend was lying inches away from.

Amara's arms looked like they'd been whipped. Her fingernails were caked with blood. Kiara knelt down beside her and pressed her lips to her forehead, grateful that Amara was breathing. She gently pushed away the other girl's hair as tears streamed down her face once again.

"I promise," she whispered, standing up and sparing one last glance at her friends, "I'll be back for you. I wish I could help you right now, but there's nothing I can do. I–" her voice caught. "All I want to do," she said, now shattering completely, "is to see you both okay, and smiling. And if not that, I just ... wish I could stay with you, lie with you, wait for our friends, possibly our saviours, to find us again. Because I believe Aidan and Krish will make it here. They will find us. I wish I could be here to greet them with you. But Advik–"

Her breath hitched when she said his name. She forced herself to look at his grotesque body. "You were right, Advik. You both ... all of you, in fact, you risked everything to save your Ordenia. Your world. And I'll be damned if I let all this go to waste. I'm sorry to leave you. And please–don't die on me."

Kiara turned away and furiously wiped her tears. She glared fiercely at what nature had put in front of her and bit back a small yelp of surprise.

There, before her, was a door. She walked towards it in a trance, mesmerized. At its base were flowers and leaves. The most stunning, vibrant flowers and leaves in colours she couldn't name. They were flowers made of laughter, pain, anger, beauty.

Branches twisted themselves along the edges and into a neat handle. Golden seeds were sprinkled all over the surface. A large keyhole cut-out had positioned itself in the centre of it all.

Kiara wrapped a shaking palm around the handle. Its twisted surface was magical. She made to force it open. But it wouldn't budge. She pulled the handle several times. She balanced her leg on the door and yanked with all her might. She threw herself at the door. She pounded on it. Over and over and over again. But it still wouldn't budge. She yelled in frustration, stuffing her finger into the keyhole. She flinched as she felt something bitingly cold ... and wet. Ice.

She knew she had to melt it, and for that she required ... *Fire.* Of course. *This* is what all of it had led to: the fire inside her was the only thing that could possibly open the door. She took a deep breath and exhaled.

And she did it again. And again. She felt her body shake with–laughter? She was unsure at first, but absolutely certain now. She was laughing hysterically, and fresh tears were streaming down her face at the same time, till she was cackling and bawling at the same time and hysteria was biting at her brain.

She sank to her knees.

Krish's hands braided the vines for what seemed like the millionth time that day. He was so bored, so tired of doing this repeatedly. All he wanted was to be back in Ordenia with Amara, with Kiara.

They could be dead for all I know.

He swallowed the lump in his throat harshly and continued braiding gloomily.

Aidan was working on another length of vines. Krish watched miserably as the sun sank behind the horizon again, marking the end of another day.

He woke up the next morning to the first rays of sunshine, and poked his companion awake. Aidan groaned.

"I'm exhausted, I've barely eaten and slept for about a minute. Let me be."

Krish was disappointed, but nothing was going to deter him. "I know, buddy. Me too. But we have to keep exerting ourselves, to keep working. That's the only way we'll make it to the others. So, I'm sorry, but we can't risk wasting more time."

Aidan rolled his eyes, but determination hardened his features. Krish offered him a hand. He took it.

The world could end for all Krish cared. He was going to reunite with his friends. And he was going to do it today.

Kiara couldn't stand erect.

She thought of her mother and her friends: they had fought too hard, sacrificed too much for Kiara to fail them now.

She sucked in a ragged breath and thrust out her hands. She reached deep inside herself and sought the fire out. She recalled every emotion to the fore, everything she'd felt since her birthday: fear, betrayal, rage, joy, sorrow. But they were all outweighed by one emotion that withstood all, the real undying flame inside her: love.

Fire erupted from her palms, dancing forward beautifully. The flames circled her, engulfed her: whispering in her ears, begging her, taunting her. She looked at them fondly. Then as she channelled them towards the door, and they started to melt the magical ice behind it, she finally let them go. And with them, all the fear and resentment within her. She felt them leaving her body, her very soul. The flames that had burned too bright had finally been put out.

The door sprang open. Taking a deep breath, Kiara stepped through it.

29

AIDAN WAS GENUINELY afraid for his life.

What terrified him more was that he was used to the feeling.

"Are we sure it won't break?" came Krish's dubious voice.

"Only one way to find out."

Aidan grinned at his friend, too widely for it to be genuine. He steadied himself with a deep breath and extended a leg forward. He was just a step from the edge. The makeshift rope was wrapped around his fingers. It had taken them a good two hours to somehow manage to loop the other end around a strong-looking tree. His hands shook. He put another leg forward and stared at his feet as they moved ahead. He stepped down onto a steep, jagged edge jutting out into the crack. He looked down, and jumped. His heart raced so loudly he was sure Krish could hear it. The wind slammed into him as he half-flew to the end of the rope. His eyes closed against the wind and dust. His legs slammed into a hard surface, and he screamed. Trying to ignore the throbbing in his legs, he opened his eyes to find himself facing the other edge of the crack. He held on to the rope with one hand, and scrambled to find purchase with the other. Following the crevices in the slope, he began climbing. His legs ached. His hands were swollen and stinging, but he urged himself to keep moving upwards. He threw his hand up and felt solid ground. Finally.

As if sensing that Aidan was too close to the end, a strong gust hit him. He yelped as he lost footing. The rope slipped out of his hand, and he tumbled backwards. He heard Krish call out his name.

Aidan's hand shot out and grabbed at the wall. He tightened his grip and risked a glance under. The wind had carried a stick with it, and it was falling fast into the chasm. His eyes followed it until he couldn't see it anymore.

That could have been me.

He swallowed, hard. His heart was positively thumping now. He pulled himself up onto the ledge, gripping the wall for dear life and swung his legs up. Regaining his hold was the trickiest part of it, which wasn't made any easier by a sinister voice in his head, echoing two haunting words: *let go.*

And part of him wanted to obey. All this struggle for what? He knew there might be a chance that he wouldn't make it; he'd prepared for the possibility. He hadn't had the time to exchange tearful farewells with his family back in Ordenia. The only friends that really mattered were with him. *Those friends need you to succeed. Don't you dare let them down.* The voice in his head wasn't his anymore. It was Kiara's.

Rejuvenated, Aidan forced his feet to still, and took a step forward. To calm himself down, he began counting his steps.

Eighteen. Nineteen. Twen–

His arm found the surface, and he hauled himself up. His feet hit solid ground. He sank to his knees in relief, putting his head in his hands. He took a few shuddering breaths. Then he turned to look at Krish, who was waving and laughing, crying and cheering.

Aidan smiled at him. He shouted, "You're up next."

Krish's smile disappeared.

Amara's head pounded. Her arms ached. Her entire body ached. She dared to open her eyes. At once, she registered the pool of sick inches away from her. Before she could begin to assess herself, she noticed Advik lying not far away. Screaming his name, she tried to get up, but gritted her teeth to keep from crying out as she collapsed again. Black spots swam in her vision. She blinked rapidly in an attempt to stay conscious and forced herself to take steady breaths.

Then she tried to turn on her side, but her arm burnt as it made contact with the ground. She yelled in agony.

"Amara!" she heard in a voice as familiar to her as her own. *Great*, she thought. *Now I'm hallucinating*. The voice came again.

"Krish?" she said, hoping beyond hope. Her voice was throaty and rough from disuse. She felt someone slump to their knees next to her. A gentle hand cradled her head and pulled it into their lap. "Krish," she realized, tears leaking out of her eyes. She felt him wipe them away.

"Yes, love," he whispered tenderly, brushing her hair out of her face. "It's me. You're going to be alright. I got you." She nodded and felt wetness on her forehead. Krish's tears.

She reached her hand out instinctively to place it on his cheek, to comfort him, but winced at the sudden movement. Her hand thudded uselessly to the side. His eyes widened as he took in her injuries. He studied her body, scanning every inch, and mumbled to himself as he took stock of the medicines he carried in his weapons belt.

"I'll be right back," he said.

She gripped his arm. "I love you."

"I love you, too," he replied, his lips brushing her cheek almost subconsciously. He hurried away. Amara tilted her head. She saw him run to Advik's side, where Aidan was already fixing him up.

"Oh my God," Krish breathed. "Is he ...?"

"He'll be okay."

"Do you need help tending to him?"

Aidan glanced at him. "I can do it, Krish," he said, wiping his mouth. In all the panic, it seemed he'd thrown up. "You go help Mary."

Amara heard the panic clearly in Krish's voice as he asked Aidan, "But ... where's Kiara?"

"I don't know."

"What do you mean?" The fear and alarm in his voice rose.

A single tear slipped out of Aidan's eye. "I can't find her. Kiara's gone."

The door closed behind her with a soft yet definitive click, launching Kiara into complete darkness.

Finally, her body gave way. Her legs buckled as she fell to the floor. Her breath came in sharp pants, and her whole body shook. In all her time being a werewolf, a Katrol, she'd never felt this way. Sure, she'd felt bitterness, rage, sorrow in more amplified amounts than she would've as a human, but she'd never felt this ... weak.

She suddenly realized she'd been thinking out loud. The word "weak" tasted bitter on her tongue. She knew she had to complete this task: this last task that would technically be a measure of her spirit. It would judge her based not on her personality, or her choices, but her as a whole. Her soul, her very being was going to be put to the test.

But she knew whatever it was, it wouldn't kill her in her sleep. So, it was there, alone in the absolute blackness, that Kiara pushed every thought out of her head and decided to let herself indulge in what might be her last slumber.

A blissful, dreamless slumber.

30

KIARA'S EYES FLUTTERED open.

She didn't know what she was looking at. It seemed like a mirror, but not quite. It couldn't possibly be a mirror for though the girl she stared at through the glass was Kiara, she was too ... perfect.

The girl in the mirror was wearing the same clothes as Kiara, but instead of being covered in mud, dirt, blood and all sorts of slime, they looked crisp and clean. Her shoes were free of all grime. Her hair was beautifully done, nowhere near the unruly nest that Kiara's hair had now become. She tugged at her shirt self-consciously. She scowled and turned to the side. The girl in the looking-glass replicated her actions perfectly. Kiara reached out to touch the glass, and gasped as sharp nails dug into her skin.

She saw her flawless reflection smile coldly at her. She shook off the grip and saw the crescent moons that had cut into her skin. She glared daggers at the other girl, desperate to mask her fear. Her cruel smile widened in response.

"What is—all this? Who are you?"

"I'm a version of yourself that you parted with mere moments ago," Kiara-but-not-really-Kiara replied, in a voice silkier and more beautiful than Kiara could ever hope to have. She flicked a delicate finger. "Modified, of course, to literally be the best version of you."

Kiara's brows rose in suspicion. "Right. And what am I supposed to do, exactly?"

"It's pretty simple," perfect Kiara said. She reached into the weapons belt slung around her waist. To Kiara's horror, she retrieved a blade so similar to Dawn even she couldn't tell the difference. "You and I ... fight to the death. No rules. All weapons, all magic," she said, and shrugged, "so it's all fair."

But Kiara's eyes were still glued to the weapon in the hands of Perfect Kiara. The other girl threw her head back and laughed, an evil sound that sent a chill up Kiara's spine.

"Meet Dusk," she said, gesturing to her dagger. The sheer wrongness of the name disgusted Kiara. It wiped away all that was significant of Dawn's name. Dawn was named so because it marked a new beginning, a fresh start, in a world so different from the one Kiara had grown up in. With new people. New opportunities. A new purpose.

To name its twin Dusk seemed inherently messed up. For what did dusk bring if not darkness?

Kiara felt sick. She unsheathed her blade. The familiarity of the blade, the comfort of holding its beautifully carved hilt again, sent a rush of warmth through her body. But she might not need the blade. What had the doppelganger said? Using magic was fair. As a desperate last resort, Kiara tried reigniting the fire inside her, tried to tug on the intense, violent emotions that had overcome her in the last few months. Nothing happened.

That's all right, Kiara thought frantically. *It always takes a few moments, doesn't it?*

But if Kiara was honest with herself, she knew it had never taken this long and she knew the reason why. She smiled at the other girl tensely, praying her expression wouldn't betray her panic. She forced her eyes shut and started to think of the anger that had ruled her since she'd first Turned, the unreasonable bitterness and vehemence she had learned to live with, but they were just ... gone. The part of her heart that had been consumed by those negative feelings was now hollow. Empty.

A realization overcame her. In melting the door, she hadn't just let go of the flames temporarily to retreat into a distant place inside her, but she'd given them up for good. And without the driving force of her murderous feelings and the ferocious, irrational urge for violence, she was no longer a Katrol.

Her heart fluttered in her chest. She was not a Katrol anymore. She'd let go of that part of her.

She'd–*shit.*

The other girl had said she was a version of Kiara that she'd parted with mere moments ago. So, while Kiara was free of being a Katrol, this other version of herself still was one. Kiara's eyes flew open just as the first ball of fire plummeted towards her. She threw herself sideways not a second too soon. The flames licked her cheeks, and the hair at the side of her head was singed. She grabbed Dawn's hilt tighter, ready for the next attack.

She expected to dodge another blast of flame, but found the other girl striding towards her, Dusk glimmering darkly in her hand. Kiara struggled to retaliate and dodged blow after blow. She tried to search for signs of weakness in her opponent but couldn't see anything but flashes of steel and fire. Her opponent moved with deadly speed and accuracy. Her body danced with her dagger, as if they were welded together, each kick, parry and strike flawless. She moved with a grace and elegance that came with practice. She had an easy demeanour about her, but it could be just a ruse.

Perspiration wet the Katrol's brow, and instead of making her look tired or sweaty, it made her glow. Her perfectly done hair whipped around, a weapon in itself. She seemed to grow stronger with every passing moment that she weakened Kiara. Her lips twisted into an icy smile. She aimed her dagger at Kiara's face. Dawn was there to meet its evil twin. Kiara pressed the blade harder. Her hands shook with the effort. She grunted in pain as Perfect Kiara replicated the act.

"You don't–have to–do this," Kiara ground out through her gritted teeth between breaths.

Her smile widened, a wicked gleam in her brown eyes. "Oh, but I do." Her weapon slashed the air and it brushed up against Kiara's cheek, drawing a few drops of blood. Kiara winced and gripped Dawn tighter. She ducked and swiftly moved to the right. Her rival tipped forward, her force working against her. Her blade jammed into the wall in front. She grabbed the hilt and tugged on it violently, but it refused to budge.

Kiara smirked. "I think it likes the wall."

Her foe glared at her with such seething hatred that Kiara could almost feel the physical force of it. She bared her teeth and hissed, and a sound that could only be described as a growl escaped her. Faster than Kiara's eyes could follow, she flew to her and pounced. Kiara's leg deflected the blow and sent her flying to the corner of the room.

"Oh," the other girl snarled with enough vehemence to cut through a diamond, "you have no idea who you're fighting against."

Her hand shot out to the blade in the wall. Physical, tangible fire lit her eyes as she tipped her head back and pulled it free.

Then she swung the dagger at Kiara's face, and Kiara swerved. The blade pinned a few strands of her hair to the wall. As she tried to break free, a ball of fire crashed down on her. She used Dawn as a shield. The other girl's eyes lit up. Kiara realized what the girl was going to do, but could do nothing but watch helplessly as Dawn caught fire in her hands. She held on to the blade as long as she could without hurting herself. A pained gasp clawed its way out of her throat.

No, she thought. *This can't be happening.*

As the heat became unbearable, what remained of her beloved weapon escaped her hands and it thudded to the floor. Its loss hit her like a ton of bricks. She sank to the floor, her hands covering her mouth as sobs built up in her throat. Though she was no longer a Katrol, the fury that burnt through her overwhelmed her and catalyzed her next movements.

She plucked Dusk out of the wall next to her, cutting some of her hair in the process. She ran towards her nemesis and jammed it through her hand, the same goddamned hand that had taken another precious thing away from her. That marked another loss that she should not be feeling at eighteen.

Her nemesis's shriek reverberated through the room. She clutched her bleeding hand and howled in agony. Tears welled up in her eyes and trickled down her cheeks. And of course, she still looked beautiful. She uttered foul curses, pain overwhelming her anger. Kiara knew she deserved it, that she was probably not even real, but her logic couldn't beat out her humanity. The anguish and torment of the voice, her own voice, tugged at her heartstrings. She sank to her knees in front of the Katrol and gently took her hands. Immediately, the vulnerability faded from her eyes. A victorious smile took its place.

She slammed the hand with the blade into Kiara's stomach. Kiara fell back, clutching her stomach. Black exploded in her vision as she was stabbed in the arm. Blood oozed out, trickling down her body slowly. Kiara screamed and wept. All she could see, all she could think about, was the excruciating pain. But she blinked the black spots out of her eyes and tried to steady herself with one hand on the wall. She tried to breathe, to concentrate on anything but the scary amount of blood she was losing.

I'm fighting myself, she thought, in an effort to distract herself. *My infinitely more evil Katrol self, but it's still me. What would I do?* Kiara almost laughed when it hit her. The other girl was towering over her, a triumphant look on her wicked face. Kiara's face.

It looked like her face was warring with itself, for her eyes were blazing with hellish fire, and the coldness of her curling lips was enough to give Kiara frostbite. But for all her bravado, it looked like she was hesitating, anticipating something.

"What are you waiting for?" Kiara asked, her voice hoarse from crying and screaming.

She frowned. "What makes you think I'm waiting for something? What makes you think," she said, pointing Dusk's blade at Kiara's neck, "that I won't just kill you right now?"

Kiara smiled up at her even as the dagger nicked the skin at her neck, causing droplets of blood to ooze out.

"You haven't done it yet," Kiara said, pushing aside the blade that looked familiar yet foreign.

Confusion flitted over the other girl's face. "What's that supposed to mean?"

"If you really wanted me dead, you would've ended my life minutes ago, before I could even ask you why you were waiting.

You wouldn't be here doing your little villain monologue for me if you ever actually intended for me to be gone."

The Katrol tensed noticeably.

"It's all right," Kiara whispered. "I couldn't do it either."

She looked puzzled. Kiara replied, "The first attack the Katrols launched on Ordenia. I knew those people were my enemies, that they would murder me without flinching if they had the chance. No matter what you are, you're a version of me. I even had two people at sword-point. But I let them go. *You* let them go."

The Katrol shook. Her eyes shuttered, and her body shook in what Kiara thought was relief. A single tear traced her porcelain cheek.

"The only way I would've actually failed this test today, is if I'd killed you," Kiara concluded. She shot the Katrol an appreciative smile. "Which would've been pretty damn hard to do."

The hint of a smile flickered on the other girl's face. And not like the heartless smiles she'd thrown at Kiara as weapons.

A real, genuine smile.

She threw Dusk away. It clattered on the floor with a harsh sound. She offered Kiara her hand. Kiara took it, and let her former self pull her up. As soon as she was able, she wrapped her uninjured arm around her and gripped her in a fierce embrace.

"We made it," Kiara said simply, her voice breaking. She felt wetness on her back, and hugged the other girl tighter, for all the times the Katrol had needed someone to comfort her. The once-robotic girl broke down hysterically. And Kiara didn't know how long she stood there; red staining not only her clothes but the other girl's too, tears streaming down her face as she heard sobs that had been her own not too long ago.

The other Kiara pulled away gently after a while. She sniffled and wiped at her face. Her once brown eyes were red and swollen. A few hiccoughs escaped her.

"Thank you," she whispered.

Kiara dabbed at her own wet face in acknowledgement. She blinked disbelievingly as her past-self dissolved slowly into a beautiful white mist.

Something fell on the floor as the mist cleared. Kiara's heart rate sped up. She couldn't believe her eyes.

It was unmistakably a small vial. The torn parchment on it read ELIXIR.

PART 4

31

KIARA SCOOPED UP the bottle in wonder.

She was numb to the wounds on her body and the tears on her cheeks. With one last look at what remained of Dawn, she turned on her heel and pushed the door open.

She was long gone by the time the last of the mist had dissipated.

Kiara stumbled out and fell to the floor. She heard a familiar voice call her name, and suddenly she was in Aidan's warm arms. His face was a picture of worry, his eyebrows scrunched together in concern. Sweat dotted his forehead, and his black curls were slick. Kiara tentatively pressed her hand to his cheek. *God, he's never looked more perfect.*

He set her down gently and tenderly tucked a lock of hair behind her ear. His eyes shone with relief and unfathomable happiness. She let her gaze linger on his face, memorizing the startling turquoise of his eyes, the sharp angles of his cheekbones, the rosiness of his lips and the curve of his neck. She heard him frantically scream for Krish.

She was startled out of her reverie and looked around. Advik. He was sitting half up and grinning softly at her.

She mouthed, *You okay?*

He nodded. *I will be. Are you?*

Kiara attempted a reassuring smile. *Me too.*

She looked up to see Aidan and Krish on their knees beside her. They were thoroughly inspecting her arm and the other cuts and scratches she had acquired that night, their expressions solemn. Despite their stoic demeanour, she could tell how joyful and relieved they were.

Kiara's arm throbbed frantically. She gritted her teeth to keep from screaming. But then she saw Amara approaching and, wordlessly, falling to her knees. She was positively beaming. Kiara didn't know how long she lay down there, surrounded by her friends. She suddenly became aware of Krish and Aidan conversing in hushed tones.

"She's okay," Krish said.

"She's not okay, Krish! Look at her arm, it's killing her!"

"I know, Aidan. Even Advik will need us to support him heavily on our way back."

"There has to be something we can do," Aidan said agitatedly, running a hand through his hair.

"Aidan," Kiara croaked.

He was startled and looked at her with enough intensity to set her insides on fire. Then his expression softened and lips parted slightly. His breath hitched when she spoke to him.

"I'll make it."

"But Kiara–"

She held out trembling fingers to him, and he took them in his own callused ones. She squeezed reassuringly and Aidan returned the pressure. Nodding at him, she pulled away. She didn't see the look of hurt flash across his features.

Just as she made to get up, she felt a sudden burning sensation in her body. She cried out and dropped to the ground, flailing about in pain.

What is happening? she thought.

Kiara fought through the stinging pain to clear her head. Her friends' concerned faces swam in and out of her vision. She tried to identify the source of the pain. *The necklace.* Her necklace was glowing. It throbbed painfully against her chest. When her quivering hands finally made to claw it open, she saw a small locket-shaped scorch mark where it had rested mere seconds ago.

No wonder my mom sounded so weak, she realized.

As soon as she managed to pry it open, a shudder of relief passed through her. Before she could let her friends know she was alright, a set of visions took ahold of her.

A Memory Orb, a distant part of her thought. Her eyes rolled back in her head and her body thrashed about as her friends' faces disappeared from her view.

Kiara, said a frantic voice. Anjali's voice. *I am so, so sorry I let you go.* What was she talking about?

I have just discovered something very disturbing. I need you to understand, love. And you mustn't respond. I know what I'm going to show you is less than ideal. But you have to know that it is too dangerous for you to respond. The stakes are too high.

Kiara's vision went black.

Then, just as abruptly as it had come, the darkness vanished, and she was left witnessing a most bizarre scene.

Anjali was walking along the panelled floor of Ordenia. A pang of longing reverberated through Kiara.

She was in a section of Ordenia Kiara had never been to. Anjali's heels clicked across the floor as she made her way to a brown sliding door. She raised her hand to knock on the door, then hesitated when she heard someone talking inside. A man was chuckling maliciously.

A familiar chuckle, Kiara realized with a start. It took a few moments to place the voice, but her eyes widened in recognition when realization dawned. President Silver.

Anjali's ears seemed to have caught something unpleasant; her lips thinned into a tight line. She pressed her ear to the door. The President cackled again. "Yes, sir, she has gone off on that wild goose chase with her little friends."

Anjali and Kiara scowled at the same time. What did he mean?

"Yes, she's been dealt with," President Silver assured whoever was on the other end. "I figured that the late Hritik's sister was a bit of a wild card. But we've altered her memory enough for her to forget it was the girl."

What did anything have to do with Rish? Hadn't her friend suffered enough already to warrant them not fiddling around in her head?

The person on the line must've offered up a compliment, for Silver said in mock modesty, "Oh, sir, you're too kind." Anjali seemed to get impatient. She slid the door open a smidge and peered in carefully.

The president was seated on a surprisingly extravagant sofa, with plush red velvet pillows and beautiful gold carvings. He was holding a simple phone and had his legs carelessly crossed over one another, draped over the edge of the sofa. His expression was ecstatic, with a dangerously gleeful smile that somehow darkened his face. His eyes glittered joyfully and he twirled his long fingers.

"We don't think Kiara and her friends can make it. The little setup is too intricate for mere children of her age to survive." A pause.

"Yes, sir, we know that Kiara and her companions are a resourceful bunch. We've made arrangements in case that happens." He listened some more to the voice on the line. "We've put together a situation that requires Kiara to use up all her fire. Even if she made it, which is extremely unlikely, she won't be a Katrol anymore once her fire is gone. The Elixir won't work on her if she's just a normal werewolf."

Kiara hadn't thought about that. *Shit.*

"Well, of course not, sir." He picked up a small, silver vial off the top of his table and brought it into the light. He looked at it in wonder.

No, Kiara thought as she squinted to read the label. *No, it can't be. That's not possible.* But it was. The little bottle that glinted in President Silver's hand was identical to the one in Kiara's fingers. The label unmistakably read, in an elegant but large script, ELIXIR.

Anjali let out a sharp wince, but thankfully the President's ears were trained on the phone. "No one in the entirety of Ordenia has any idea that what she and her pesky little friends have gone off on is a fake quest for a fake Elixir."

Kiara was sure her ears were failing her. Fake quest? Fake Elixir?

"It should take a few more days. With Kiara not being a Katrol anymore, and not even being here, now should be the perfect time to strike. Yes, I have the Elixir in my possession. William handed it over to me a couple months ago. Not like it'll be of any use to Ordenia anyway, now that their only faithful little Katrol has been neutralized."

A wicked laugh followed.

"We've made this new set of hurdles for Kiara and her friends difficult enough that we will be spared their nuisance for a good while, but easy enough that Kiara will most likely survive." A long pause ensued. "It's been a pleasure working with you too, sir."

Anjali waited a few moments before knocking on the door and entering. All the colour drained out of the president's face when he saw her. His casual grace was replaced with panic and genuine fear as he invited her in. She resumed the conversation like everything was normal, speaking of Ordenian matters that could not bother Kiara less.

Kiara drowned out the conversation, her teary eyes wide in horror, her mouth open. The necklace stopped throbbing. She got up so abruptly that she banged her head into Aidan's.

"Ow!" he complained, rubbing his forehead. "What was that? You looked like you were having a fit or something. Are you okay?"

Kiara looked at her friends.

"You guys have to trust me on this. I'll explain on the way, okay?"

"On the way where?"

"We're going home. *Now.*"

"So, all this was nothing more than an illusion? We risked our lives for nothing?" Aidan asked, not for the first time.

They were going back the same way they came, across the rope the two boys had braided, the mermaid-filled water, the tornado-free land. But none of those places seemed to want to attack them now. The crack in the earth sewed itself together when they had to cross. The water was peaceful and almost eerily calm.

Advik was leaning heavily on Aidan, an arm slung across his shoulder. It was definitely challenging, but Aidan wasn't complaining. After all, he wasn't the one whose leg was so utterly ... broken. They stopped ever so often to clean out his wound and replace the bandages with fresh ones.

Kiara was leading the group while narrating what she'd seen through the Memory Orb Anjali had sent her. Her voice was surprisingly steady as she elucidated everything in detail, taking and responding to all their questions patiently.

Aidan knew her well enough to see the cracks in her composed exterior. Her hands had a slight tremor to them. Beads of sweat lined her forehead. Her eyes were slightly widened, as if she herself was still processing all that had happened. The urge to grab her and wrap her in his arms was almost overwhelming. Aidan wanted to hold her, to whisper in her ears that they would be alright. That they'd make it. Together. He wanted to brush his lips over her forehead, her cheeks, her lips ...

He tore his eyes away from her and diverted his thoughts. If what she was saying was true, then a battle was coming. One deadlier and with higher stakes than any they'd fought before.

He needed to keep his head straight. But when he thought about her, damn, those brown eyes were all he could think about.

Kiara was nodding. She looked at Advik unhappily. She slowed her pace to walk alongside Aidan and Advik. She looked over at them with such concern, such softness that it was all Aidan could do to keep from kissing her.

"How're you holding up?" she said softly to Advik, firmly keeping her gaze averted from Aidan's.

He smiled meekly at her. "I'm getting better. It's this guy who deserves your concern, really," he said, gesturing at Aidan. "He's the one who's been practically carrying me for, what, three hours now?"

Aidan patted Advik on the back appreciatively. "You took the hit for us. It's the least I can do."

Aidan felt Kiara tense next to him. She was staring at him in that special way: her eyes scanning every inch of him, lips slightly parted, hair flowing softly behind her. And even in her battered, filthy state, she'd never looked more beautiful. Aidan's heart fluttered as he met her gaze.

"How long will he take to recover?" Kiara asked, and Aidan deflated slightly.

He stared intently at his shoes while answering, "We'll hopefully be back in Ordenia in less than a week. With frequent pitstops, adequate rest and constant medication, he should be alright by the time we reach."

Kiara loosened up a little as she exhaled. Then she looked straight into Aidan's eyes. "And how are you?"

How was he?

How *was* he? How could he answer that? Looking at her set him on fire. Thinking of her broke his heart, as did looking at the friend leaning on his shoulder. The anticipation of the inevitable war filled him with an unexplainable dread. But the worst of them all? The worst was the wait. The frustrating journey home. The knowledge that his people were probably being slaughtered and there was nothing he could do but go on, and keep going. It killed him that his loved ones had to take the weight of the war, and that he was not there to fight alongside them.

"I'm fine," was all he said.

The way Kiara nodded at him made it seem like she didn't believe him one bit. Like she saw through his bravado to his insecurities, his fears, his hopes, dreams and desires. And most of all, that she understood.

Ever since the day of their kiss, Kiara had been overly cautious not to touch him. She'd always purposely walk at a distance, using their friends as a barrier between Aidan and herself. She was careful to avoid any accidental touches even when they were merely walking together.

But now, she stood on her toes and planted a gentle kiss on his cheek. He flushed instantly. His skin sparked and tingled where it came in contact with her soft lips. It sent a small jolt up his spine. She glanced at him once more as she patted Advik's arm gently and went on to join the rest of their friends.

Aidan put his hand to his cheek where Kiara's lips had been seconds ago. The feeling of them was almost ... haunting.

The bloody lip-shaped stain lingered on his cheek for a long time.

32

AMARA COULDN'T SLEEP.

Not for lack of trying. She'd practically forced her eyes shut, and was squeezing them so tight it hurt. Her head was pounding with the after-effects of everything that had happened. But most of all, what really kept her awake was the revelation that all this—everything they'd done—was futile. Fake.

And even if it hadn't been, even if what they'd retrieved had actually been the Elixir and not a replica, Kiara wasn't a Katrol anymore. Even if they narrowed down the location of the genuine Elixir, they couldn't do anything about it.

Though it was not in the best interests of Ordenia, a rather large part of Amara was very happy for her friend. She'd seen how disgusted Kiara had been with her own nature, and how strongly she'd yearned to be normal. To be ordinary. And now, she was.

Smiling, Amara finally let sleep sweep her away.

A blinding light woke Krish up the following morning. His slumber hadn't been as restful as he'd hoped. On the contrary, it had been fitful and sweaty. And mosquito-filled. *Really* mosquito-filled.

He hastened to get up, the grass poking his skin. He pulled up his shirt to find small scratches and mosquito bites across his entire torso, and groaned. He ran his hand through his hair. The sun was nothing short of glaring at them.

Amara was beginning to stir. Her eyes flew open, and she fixed the blazing sun with a fierce glower, and scratched at her legs, taking in her surroundings. Krish caught her gaze and, together, they gently nudged the others awake.

Krish was unsurprised to find that they all looked just as restless as him. Their expressions were almost identical: grim and dismal. They exchanged gloomy 'good morning's and 'did you sleep well's, then wordlessly fell into the rhythm of walking home.

His stomach was growling ferociously, and from the sound of it, he wasn't the only one who was starving. When was the last time they'd eaten?

He watched Aidan quickly clean and dress Advik's wound. As he snuck a glance at it, he was genuinely impressed by how far Advik had come.

Luckily, Aidan had kept the map in his weapons belt, so he was the one who led the grumpy group homeward.

According to the map, they were now painfully close.

Aidan's stomach almost revolted in anticipation, but he didn't have anything in it to throw up. He thought he was going to turn delirious from hunger. Advik was now leaning only ever so slightly on Krish's shoulder. His leg had healed impressively fast, but Aidan worried that Advik would want to take part in whatever was brewing in Ordenia, and the injury would not fare well under intense combat.

So, he waited until Krish and Advik caught up with him and offered them a weak smile. Krish's lips puckered up and Advik just nodded.

"Hey, Advik, how's the leg doing?"

Advik grinned. "I walked a few steps on my own today." His happiness was infectious.

Aidan couldn't help smiling. "That's great, buddy. Uh, listen, when we get back to Ordenia, which should be–" he checked his map "–any minute now, judging by the density of the woods, there ... uh ... might have been an attack from the Katrols."

Advik furrowed his brows. "I know."

"And not to dampen your spirit or anything, but I–"

"–want me to sit this one out?" Advik finished. Aidan's expression turned apologetic. "You're right."

"I–what? So, you're not going to put yourself at risk till your leg's healed?"

"I promise when we get back to Ordenia, I'll find a place to rest my leg and avoid using it as much as I can. You've brought me this far. I trust your judgement. I'll do what I can for Ordenia, but without having to physically exert myself. I'm still part of the fight that way."

Aidan heaved a huge sigh of relief. "I thought I was going to have to fight you on this."

Advik chuckled. "I'm not Kiara," he said, looking at him suggestively, and wiggled his eyebrows.

"No," Aidan said, his eyes darting to Kiara. "You're not."

Kiara's brown hair was laughing in the sunlight. Her twinkling eyes were so startling that Aidan took a sharp breath. Her brows were furrowed with worry in that adorable way that made him want to sweep her into his arms. He averted his gaze to look ahead, but nearly dropped his map. His mouth fell open, and his body tingled with nerves.

"What is it?" Advik enquired, noticing Aidan's awestruck face.

"Guys!" he called out.

Kiara turned to him, her hair fluttering behind her in a stunning arc. "Yeah?"

He lost his train of thought. He shook his head and slapped his face.

"We're here."

Amara's hands trembled on the doorknob. She didn't want to open that door.

Because it would show them what destruction their home was going through. Because it would show them whether their worst fears had come true. Because, potentially, there was an unbeatable army of Katrols awaiting their return on the other side of the door. An army against which they didn't even have a fighting chance.

Krish gently took her head in his hands and pressed a gentle kiss on her lips. She kissed him back slowly, and leaned her forehead against his.

"I love you," she whispered. She felt him nod against her forehead.

"I love you, too."

In a moment that felt painfully slow, yet too fast to comprehend, he put his hand on her shaking one and pulled open the door.

She put one foot into the door, and felt Krish moving with her. She felt her friends' anxious eyes on them. Krish and Amara took a few more steps together, Amara's quivering palm against Krish's sweaty one.

It seemed perfectly safe.

She called her friends in, relieved. Krish turned to her with fear in his eyes as they entered. Amara took a second to look at her surroundings–it seemed eerily perfect.

Too safe.

Her mouth flew open to shout out a warning to her friends, but her words were strangled as she felt corded arms snaking around her neck. She choked. She bared her teeth, preparing to bite into the attacker's hands when she felt something rough go over her head, and cursed as something hard and heavy hit her head.

Black spots swam in her vision. She attempted to blink them away.

Why try? the voice inside her chided. *You're frail and the lack of food has made you delirious and weak. Give in, Amara. Give in.*

She struggled harder to regain her sight. Her eyes fluttered feebly.

I will not give up, she swore fiercely.

But in the end, the voice was right. Her body betrayed her and the world went black.

Kiara's head pounded. Her instincts had protested violently against stepping into Ordenia. Even as she watched Krish and Amara walk in first and declare it safe, the homely feeling she'd come to associate with Ordenia in the brief time that she'd been acquainted with it had dissolved into the air.

She heard Amara's muffled gag, and her heart nearly stopped.

"Mary?" she whispered, looking for the girl who had been in front of her not a second ago.

"Mary!" She knew she was going against the training she'd been given, to stay calm and think logically, as she screamed frantically for her friend. Her voice betrayed all the emotions playing through her head; an overwhelming sense of foreboding, a strangely unfamiliar panic, and a deep, indescribable fear that she'd never felt before.

Her voice cracked traitorously. She snapped her head from side to side, eyes scanning every inch of her surroundings for the direction of Amara's voice. She heard a soft rustling of leaves to her right, so soft that she might have missed it if she hadn't been on high alert.

Her head whipped around to face it, arm flying instinctively to the empty sheath where Dawn had rested not too long ago. A foreign face appeared in front of her.

Her arm threw itself forward, as if on its own, her fist coming in hard contact with bumpy skin. Her knuckles split from the force of the punch. The stranger in front of her broke into a wicked smile as Kiara realized her mistake a heartbeat too late.

A large, heavy object hit her skull at the same time that a sack was thrown over her head. She didn't have the time or the energy to cry out as her vision blackened with a strange but immovable darkness.

It could have been seconds or weeks later when Kiara's eyes reluctantly batted open. Her head felt like it had been split open. She felt something wet in her hair. Her eyes might as well have stayed closed, for she could still see nothing. She tried to hold in the sob that had been building in her throat, but it broke free, the traitor.

She immediately felt movement around her, and before she could fully comprehend what was happening, light burst upon her eyes. She squinted, struggling to adjust to the searing brightness of the sun. She tipped her head back, absorbing the sunshine.

Her momentary pleasure was immediately replaced by horror.

She was tied to a chair, ropes bound so tight they dug into her skin, drawing blood. And she wasn't the only one. Three identical chairs were to her left, one to her right. Three of her friends were tied to her left. They were still unconscious, their heads drooping. She scanned each of them, the reassuring rise and fall of their chests made her throat close up with emotion.

On the chair to her right, a pair of piercing turquoise eyes were looking at her in alarm and relief.

"Kiara," Aidan choked out, his tongue parched and voice raw with disuse and ... feeling? Desperation?

Kiara's heart skipped a few beats. She inched her chair carefully towards him, making sure it didn't creak. She then tried to extricate her arms from the mess of ropes behind her till her nails bloomed red. She sighed, and rested her head on his shoulder. He let out a strangled sound before brushing his lips lightly against her hair. Kiara shivered at the contact. She retracted her head from the steadiness of his shoulder and boldly looked into his eyes. He returned her stare, lips parting.

She didn't think before tilting her head up and making to seal the distance between their lips. Her body tingled in anticipation when–

Creak. Creaaaakkkkk.

One of the chairs behind Kiara groaned. She stifled her own frustrated groan, taking one last glance at Aidan. He was swallowing hard, eyes glittering with desire and disappointment.

He cleared his throat loudly. "Mary," he said, all annoyance dissolving instantly from his face. "You okay?"

Amara looked deathly pale, almost green. Sweat glistened all over her body. She was trembling, and a soft moan escaped her lips.

Kiara's panicked voice reached her ears as if from a different place, another time. "Food!" Kiara cried, taking in Amara's state, her voice cracking. "She needs food, water, anything!"

Aidan shot her a resigned glance. "Kiara–" he began.

"No, Aidan," she commanded. She knew what he would tell her. These captors, most likely Katrols, wouldn't have kidnapped them just to give in to their demands later. They wouldn't have taken them hostage if they wanted to treat them lavishly. But Kiara didn't want to listen to reason. Her friend looked frighteningly gaunt, and she needed to get something into her stomach.

"Water!" Kiara repeated, desperate tears streaming down her face. "Get her some food, somebody, anything!"

Krish awoke abruptly. "Why are you yelling for food, Sharma?" he asked tiredly.

His eyes drifted to Amara's face. He went white. He opened his mouth and joined Kiara's chants. "Help! Please, anyone!" they shouted.

"Now, now," said a voice, tutting. "We'll get you food, children. If you would just stop that incessant noise ..."

Kiara's blood boiled as the figure emerged from the shadows. President Silver, his sneer more evident than ever, stalked through their ranks.

Advik stirred. His eyes snapped open, red and animalistic. He took in the situation, hatred sparking in his eyes as his gaze fell on the towering president.

"You bastard," he spat.

Silver had the nerve–the nerve–to chuckle in delight, as if he were sharing a cup of tea with a friend.

"That's quite a sharp tongue you've got there, young man. I'm afraid I will have to politely disagree with the sentiment."

Advik growled at him. Kiara snarled as she clawed at the ropes, her nails bloody and broken.

"It was you," Aidan's lips curved in loathing. "Kiara already informed us, but you–all this time, we were out there risking our lives for Ordenia, on your orders–"

"Let me stop you there, Mr Moonstone. That's all the more reason that this is all so deliciously twisted. You didn't put your necks on the line for Ordenia. You were just children–children wanting desperately to believe they're important."

"This was all just a wild goose chase then?" Amara said, ice steeling her voice and fury keeping it steady.

The President smiled cruelly. "Now that," he said, bursting with barely controlled glee, "is not for me to reveal."

"So now what, weren't you–the what–the mastermind of this–this operation?" Kiara said, eyebrows furrowing in confusion.

"While I'm most flattered, Ms Sharma, I'm afraid I was just a means to an end. Although I'm sure you will soon recognize the, ah, mastermind, as you said, behind this operation. For now, my orders are to comply with your demands, and frankly alarming protests for food. Our master will be here in a few short days' time."

"I'd rather die than eat something from you," Krish bellowed defiantly.

"Admirable as your bravery and loyalty is, I hate to break it to you that one of your number is already dying," he said with a pointed glance at Amara.

Her bravado had leaked out of her, and she was bent over in her chair, retching dryly. Krish's shoulders slumped.

Desperation coloured his voice as he said, "Now."

"Not so fast," President Silver said. "There are certain regulations you must agree to before–"

"Agreed," the four of them instantly exclaimed. They were intently watching Amara, who'd gone scarily pale.

"Kids," President Silver said with a dramatic sigh. "Always so quick to give up everything for your loved ones."

"Wouldn't you?" Kiara said, not sure why she was curious.

"Oh, I've long since learnt that in order to gain power and status, people are not worth getting attached to. If you have nobody to love, you have nothing to lose."

Part of Kiara wanted to roll her eyes–such a cliched villain line. But another thought overpowered her: if he had no weakness, how would they defeat him?

Another, more sinister musing followed. If they couldn't defeat him, how were they going to take down his master?

Kiara swallowed, willing whatever was left in her stomach to remain there.

Krish wasn't very pleased with the 'regulations' Silver had put into place.

For the six days that followed, they were tied up in their chairs. If they had to go to the bathroom, they were allowed only one at a time, flanked by a minimum of three hulking men. Then too, they were patted down thoroughly, having to strip down to a minimum amount of clothing.

All their weapons and supplies lay in a useless heap on the ground, frustratingly close yet painfully far away. Krish's hands twitched to get his hands on any of them, even a gun, which was his least preferred weapon.

They were blindfolded twice a day, and rough hands shoved tasteless food down their throats. On the first day, Kiara had spat on the face of one of the people in defiance. The scars of the aftermath of her revolt stood out on her bronze face.

Thankfully though, Amara was growing healthier day by day. Colour had returned to her face, and her hollow cheekbones were gradually filling out. She'd stopped hurling up her guts thrice a day, and her forehead had returned to its normal temperature, her voice to its steady sweetness.

Krish knew how they were being treated wasn't fair. It wasn't half as bad as he'd thought it would be, but it was still brutal. He hadn't felt his legs in days, and his hands were raw and bloody from trying to outmanoeuvre the ropes. But damn, if he wouldn't do it a thousand times over just to see the splashes of pink on Amara's cheeks again.

"Blindfolds on," said the cheerful voice of President Silver.

Krish gritted his teeth as someone fastened the fold of darkness around his eyes. He didn't know what they were so afraid of them seeing, and not for a lack of pondering about it. Callused hands stuffed a bland meal down his throat. He spluttered and choked, but they kept going. Krish blinked back painful tears.

"Children," the hateful voice boomed.

What he wouldn't give to strangle the person he'd once so admired.

"I have received confirmation that Mr–our leader–will be arriving on this fortuitous day. Though most of you are already familiar with him."

Krish hadn't stopped wondering about the identity of this mysterious master. Much as he racked his brains, he couldn't figure out who it could be.

It could've been minutes, or was it hours later, that Krish finally heard approaching footsteps. A lot of footsteps. Sweat slithered down his spine, chilling him to the bones. His slick hands quivered.

"Ah, Albert," said a man's voice from behind Krish's back. He tried twisting his head to the speaker, but to no avail.

Besides, why did Krish recognize that voice? He heard a thump. Dear God. Were the two embracing and patting each other on the back? This was really not the time for a celebratory villain reunion. Krish shuddered.

President Silver came into his peripheral vision. He drew closer, another man following. If Krish had thought President Silver's usual attire was strangely ominous, it was nothing compared to the dreary ensemble this mysterious stranger had on. A large maroon coat swished behind him as he walked. He wore a black fedora, covering his dark locks. A hint of bronze skin peeked through a dark blue blazer sleeve. He slowly took the hat off. Krish paled. Sweat ran down his back, cooling his hot skin.

How had he not known? Amara and Aidan exchanged confused but curious glances. Advik's mouth dropped open, and he was swallowing deeply as if trying not to throw up.

But Kiara ... Kiara.

Her intense shock took a micro-second to turn into a deluge of tears. And then she was weeping in earnest, her body wracked with violent sobs. She shook her head over and over again, as if willing herself to wake up from this nightmare.

"No, no, no!" she yelped, her voice thick with tears and breath barely catching.

She finally croaked out, "Papa?"

33

"WHAT?" WAS ALL Aidan could muster.

This man standing in front of them ... the puppeteer orchestrating everything ... the reason for Hritik's and countless others' deaths ... the reason for all this suffering ... the reason for Kiara crying like that ... was Kiara's father?

Aidan looked away from Kiara. He felt he could hear her heart crack as she coughed to gain control of herself. His palms clenched into fists.

Kiara's father or not, he would kill this man if it was the last thing he did. Or better still, hold him down as Kiara delivered the fatal blow.

"Why?" Kiara whispered, her voice cracking with rage and despair.

"It's good to see you, too, Kia," Mr Sharma said. "Krish, Advik ... always a pleasure. I don't believe I've been acquainted with you two lovely children," he said, his voice calm and buttery as he turned to Amara and Aidan.

"I'm Manohar Sharma." He paused expectantly, as if waiting for an introduction. When he got none, he barked a laugh. "Kia, you asked me why. Why I did all this. Well, where do I begin?

"I–I'm not a young man. You remember the party I had a year ago for my forty-fifth? The simple answer is–being a

Katrol has never been easy. Being discriminated for something so beyond your control cuts deep into your soul. Knowing that you cannot trust anyone around you, or find meaningful relationships, because you must keep everyone at an arm's length is the worst thing one can experience. You know what it's like Kiara—to look people in the eye and see fear and disgust, to be discarded as feral.

"But does anyone of you know? I was afraid to be dismissed as an outsider, so I went to extraordinary lengths to disguise myself as one of you." He snarled, pointing at Kiara's friends. "I suffered through my nightmares alone, hid myself on full moon nights, as a young Katrol, to make sure I didn't hurt anyone and wore brown contacts, even when I went to sleep, so that no one could see the monster in me."

Aidan's heart squeezed. He couldn't help but feel a twinge of sympathy for the man in front of him. He knew this man had done despicable, unspeakable things—and Aidan probably didn't even know the worst of it—but everyone deserved equality. Everyone deserved a little empathy. And Manohar was right. Aidan would never know how it felt. Manohar turned his head to see Amara trembling, her lips white from pressing against each other, to keep her tears from spilling over.

"And when I Turned—when I walked through that door into Ordenia—I was beyond ecstatic. In front of my eyes lay a fresh start. A world I believed was free of discrimination. Alas, I was sorely mistaken.

"For not only had discrimination crept into Ordenia, a supposed haven for werewolves, but these people had a definite clan they oppressed—the Katrols. Yet another chunk of the world's population that was punished, hunted, killed for something they had no control over."

His bitter laugh chilled Aidan to the bones.

"See, that's the thing about people. Something new, something unconventional, something out of their norm hits them, and their first reaction is to panic. To attack. To eradicate this terrifying unknown and let the world continue with its 'normal'. What about those of us whom Ordenia deems abnormal?" Aidan felt a chill run down his spine.

"So here I was," Manohar Sharma continued. "A wide-eyed, innocent, eighteen-year-old, thinking things would finally be all right. That I'd finally be on equal footing with everyone else. And in less than two weeks, those dreams crashed and burned. I was out of here and making changes before your mother Turned. And I truly loved her, your mother. But acting on those feelings would lead to me revealing that I was a Katrol, and give up all I would go on to build, all for one woman. But I stayed in Mumbai. I stayed so that I could be in close contact with my spies in Ordenia. So I could actively change the system from the werewolf capital of the world.

"I had to set aside my love for your mother to accomplish all this. And it was dreadful at first, to be in love with her, to marry her, when I was training myself to throw all those feelings and all my heartbreak out of the window. But I look around now, and I can't help but think it was worth it. And then of course, Anjali became pregnant with you. And suddenly I had another purpose in life. A child, my own child to support my cause. The path to this point had been dark, merciless and unyielding. I spent longer than you would believe, did worse things than you could possibly imagine, to get to where I am today.

"What started as a group of three brave kids–Manohar, Dmitry and William–has become something so beautiful, so meaningful, so powerful."

Dmitry walked up to Manohar and put a hand on his shoulder. His eyes were shimmering with pain for his friend.

They stood like that for a few moments, until Kiara managed, "How?" The word was more command than query.

Feeling disappeared from Manohar's eyes. They were ... Kiara's eyes.

"You really thought," President Silver sniggered, giving Manohar time to compose himself, "that that was the actual set of blockages that Sylvia designed relentlessly alongside hundreds of genius minds till her dying day? Did you really think that five children could not only get through it and retrieve the most potent magical concoction ever made, but also make it out alive and–well, not unscathed," he crooned, his gaze locked on Advik's destroyed leg. "We sacrificed a large number of our brave warriors, year after year, trying to get through the impossible hurdles. And finally, it was William, of course, who managed. It is no surprise to us. His genius is profound. He led fifty of our greatest soldiers, potioneers and swordsmen to procure the Elixir. He was among the fourteen people who managed to make it out alive. In fact, I collected the Elixir from him just a few months ago."

"And what was all that, what we all went through?" Krish growled, voice shimmering with unveiled contempt.

"Oh, just a little something we let our potioneers have fun with. It was all little more than an illusion. Kia, believe me when I say it has been the hardest thing I have ever had to do, to not recruit you for our cause the day you Turned," said Manohar.

"And I tried when you were fourteen years old, I really tried," he continued. "But you wouldn't listen. You started screaming and crying and throwing tantrums. What else could I have done? I had no choice but to erase your memory. I–I wanted to plead my case to you so badly–to turn you to our side just as I'd Turned you from girl to wolf–"

A harsh sound tore through the shocked silence that followed. Kiara was clawing at the ropes around her hands, kicking the legs of her chair harder than ever before, trying violently to break free. The blow of the betrayal had clearly broken her.

"The whole purpose of the course we cooked up," continued Manohar, oblivious to his daughter's heartbreak, "was to transform Kiara from a Katrol to a regular werewolf, and rid her of her extraordinary abilities as one. I knew that even though I am your father, you have this skewed view of goodness that might prevent you from agreeing with me. That frustratingly moral part of you could have stolen the Elixir from Silver's office–"

"Now, now," Silver interrupted, his lips curling unpleasantly at what his friend had let slip.

"–and utterly destroyed our army, and we can't have that," Manohar continued. He then flushed and looked to Silver, running an embarrassed hand through his hair, clearly apologetic.

"What do you want, Papa?" Kiara said, her voice devoid of the pain that had taken over her face moments ago.

"I want you to join me, Kiara, and I ask but once. Now, I know you're not a Katrol any longer, but we will make room for you. We'll welcome you with open arms, and make you feel at home and safe, like you belong."

Aidan gazed at Kiara. His heart sank. She looked like she was contemplating it, and Aidan couldn't blame her. He couldn't tell her what to do, he couldn't be selfish. What her father was offering her was infinitely better than what her position in Ordenia had been. Though it would inevitably break Aidan, he couldn't selfishly deny her the one shot she had at equality. At freedom. At a chance to change the world. His throat tightened as Kiara made to answer with fiery passion in her eyes.

"I would rather die," she spat.

Manohar clicked his tongue disapprovingly, something deceptively like hurt clouding his eyes. "I will give you till tomorrow morning to reconsider."

"Why?" Kiara said defiantly, tears drying and hardening her expression. "What's tomorrow morning?"

"Tomorrow morning," Manohar said, "we strike."

He turned away, only to look back and say, "I want you to think about it, Kiara. I plan on changing our world forever. I'd much rather do it with you by my side. But if you can't–just remember, I detached myself from your mother. I don't think it'll be much harder to do it with you."

And just like that, he walked away, not glancing back to see his daughter's face crumple.

Krish's eyes turned involuntarily to Kiara. All of them were now staring at her. Amara gave Kiara a tentative smile, but Kiara's eyes had darkened too much to return it.

"I should've known," Kiara said. "I should've known all along."

"No," Aidan said, more commanding than consoling. "There's no way."

"He fooled us, too, you know," Krish offered.

"For years," Advik added.

"But he is my father," Kiara choked. "All those damn fishing trips he went on–they were always around the full moon. All the times I'd heard wolves howling in the forest, it was him and his goddamn army. And God only knows what he's done to innocents to get here."

The pain in Kiara's voice seemed to stir Aidan. For within moments, his hands were out of those inescapable ropes and cupping Kiara's cheeks gently. Her eyes shone. Krish looked away, feeling like he was intruding on a private moment.

When he looked back, he saw Kiara's jaw drop to the floor the same second that Aidan seemed to realize he'd escaped the ropes. He'd broken free.

He stared at his bloodied but free hands in wonder. He–he'd escaped!

Krish clamped his lips together tightly to suppress a shout as Aidan moved his shaking hands to undo his bindings. And then Amara's. Advik's. Kiara's.

"Advik," Krish whispered urgently, having regained his composure first, "you have to go. Run. Now."

Advik shifted uncomfortably. Krish could see the calculations running through his mind.

"Advik," Krish repeated. "Go."

Aidan put his hand on Advik's shoulder, rougher than he normally would. "I know it'll be terrifying being inside, not knowing if we survived, and hell, if you told me to do it, I probably wouldn't have, I couldn't have."

"Really helpful," Amara muttered under her breath.

"But out here, you'd be a liability at best, a hostage at worst. And I swear, Advik, this isn't one of those jobs where we feed you shit about you doing the 'most important job', because there is no most important job. We need you, Advik. Useful or not, we need you."

Advik's face softened as he nodded at his friends, got up weakly and limped slowly out of sight.

Krish felt his throat go tight and cleared it quickly. "What do we do now?"

"What Advik did," Amara replied. "We run like hell."

34

KIARA FORCED HER mind to focus on her flying feet as she fled like a criminal escaping a crime scene. She wouldn't have been able to handle herself otherwise.

Krish kept pace on her left. She knew he could have easily overtaken her, and appreciated him all the more for that. To her right, Aidan was at her heels, his face hollower and gaunter than she'd ever seen it. The starvation they'd undergone had carved its way into his face. She felt the ghost of his tender hands on her skin and relished the feeling. If these were to be her last moments, she was going to allow herself that pleasure.

She blinked rapidly, dissipating tears at the thought, as she looked back and forth between the two boys that mattered most to her.

"Guys," Amara panted as she fell back. Kiara bolted to catch her mid-air, just in time, as her eyes rolled back and she lost consciousness.

"I definitely heard someone," Kiara whispered.

It had been a good three days since Amara had passed out. The other three had managed to hoist her body to a safe spot hidden in the bushes to which Aidan had led them. They had taken turns to forage water and food from their rooms and the kitchen at Headquarters, leaving one person behind to look after Amara and another to defend them in case they were found.

All through the day, sometimes even bleeding into the night, they heard battle cries, howls for mercy, soft sighs of relief. They had all taken shifts, true, but not one of them had managed to get a minute of sleep.

Amara was sitting up now, her complexion deathly pale. Krish held a glass of water as she sipped, his hands steady but eyes ablaze.

Kiara glanced around. "That's weird. I–I don't see anyone."

"You sure? I swear I did."

Kiara nodded. "Aidan?"

"Yeah?"

"What are we doing?"

"What do you mean?" he asked, looking confused.

"The Elixir we hunted down was fake. We don't have the real one. It's apparently in Silver's office, as my dad let slip. Even if, by some miracle, we did have it, I'm not a Katrol anymore. I can't do anything about it. We have no idea where Advik is, whether he's okay. What if he's dead somewhere and we don't even know? And why are we hiding out here? We should be out there, fighting. We can't ignore the things we've been hearing. We know there's a battle going on. We know their army is so much more powerful than ours. Ordenia will be under their control, and Mom–this will shatter her and I–"

"Hey, hey," Aidan said gently, drawing her into his arms. He stroked her hair and rubbed slow circles on her back. Her breathing gradually slowed, her eyes shut tight against his chest. She pulled back and turned her face up to look at him. His eyes were open, vulnerable. Beyond that, she could see he was terrified. His eyes glittered with palpable fear. She felt a rush of tenderness towards him, and cupped his face in her hands, allowing him to lean into her touch. She felt his guard go down.

It was the wrong moment.

A twig snapped behind them. Aidan's face instantly hardened, and he unsheathed his blade. A second too late.

The gunshot rang through Kiara's ears.

She screamed, her eyes instinctively closing. She didn't feel anything, but could smell blood. Its metallic scent filled her nostrils. She heard Aidan's ragged breathing.

Aidan.

She forced her eyes open. There he was, on the ground. His shirt had ridden up, and his hand was covering a part of his stomach. Tears were falling from his blue-green eyes. He was shuddering in pain.

This could not be happening. Aidan had not been shot. Surely she was dreaming. Surely she'd just passed out due to lack of food or rest. Surely she'd open her eyes and be back just a few metres away, with a recovering Amara and her best friend. Aidan's palm shook as he moved it away from his wound.

It was a deep, dark scarlet. Reality came crashing down around her. In a second, Kiara fell on her knees next to him and took his hand. Tears continued to stream down the sides of his face. She wiped them away.

"Shh," she whispered. "Shush, my love. You're going to be just fine. I promise you."

She tore a small piece of her already tattered t-shirt and pressed it to the wound. The smell of blood nearly overwhelmed her. She finally looked up to see the person who'd put Aidan in so much pain.

Her father stood over her, an elegant silver pistol gleaming in his hands. He was ... he was ... *smiling.*

"Kia," he said. "Kia, sweetie."

Hearing him call her Kia, a nickname that had been reserved only for him ever since she could remember, was the last straw. Her stomach flipped and she heaved up the pitiable amount of food and water she'd managed to scavenge in the last three days.

Her father was instantly next to her, holding her hair back, murmuring soothingly.

"Papa?" she croaked.

"Yes, honey?"

"I'm never going to forgive you, you know that, right? I'm never going to stop resisting you. I'm never going to stop fighting."

"I take this to mean you will not come quietly?" Manohar said, but it was not really a question.

"Come quietly?" Kiara laughed hysterically.

"Stop running from me, Kia. You're never going to get far enough, fast enough. Just join me. Join us."

She said nothing, just continued laughing.

"Perez?"

"Yes, sir."

"The injection."

"But, sir–"

"He is dying," Manohar said suddenly, turning back to his daughter. "Your, ah, friend, is he? Your *special* friend will be dead in minutes if you don't let us tend to him."

Kiara turned her defiant face to Aidan. His face had gotten paler, his breathing slower and heavier, eyes red-rimmed. All her fire fizzled out.

He opened his mouth and choked, "Kiara ..."

"Don't you dare," she whispered. "Don't give me the 'I'll die, but don't give in' hero monologue." She managed a weak chuckle. "Never liked heroes much."

She turned to her father. "Fix him. Please, I'll do anything you want."

"You won't resist me or Mr Perez here?"

"I won't."

"I have your word?"

"Do I have yours?"

"Yes."

"Then, I promise," she said. A sob wrenched from her. "Fix. Him. Now."

Manohar nodded. He called out a few names, and Kiara faintly registered people in white coats surrounding them, surrounding him. There was a great clinking of glass, rubbing of gloves and opening of bottles as the medics moved around to repair what Kiara's father had damaged.

"They'll take care of him," Manohar reassured her. "Your dagger, Kia?"

"It's gone," Kiara said. "Your fake Elixir hunt destroyed it."

"I'm sorry to hear that."

"You're ... sorry? You–who just shot an innocent boy to get my guard down, to get me to cooperate with you–you're sorry about a dagger? I don't believe you."

Manohar nodded. "You promised you wouldn't protest," he said resignedly. "This is just going to knock you unconscious for a bit, okay? Just for a bit."

He held out a syringe, and carefully put the needle through her skin. She heard him saying, "Go find the other two, Smith. They should be around here. I don't think injuring one of them will be necessary. They've both seen better days."

The darkness flooded in, and with it, momentary relief.

35

ADVIK'S OWN BREATHING echoed through the dank, hollow room, the only thing giving him company in this solitude.

He leaned his head against the wall, allowing his eyes to close but never letting his mind wander. Since leaving his friends' side a few days ago, he had stayed hidden within Ordenia. On the first day, he had broken into his room after distracting the guards. He'd then cleaned up his wound and rebandaged it. He'd wolfed down the snacks stacked in his pantry, and fetched a backpack to stuff it with water, food and medicine to last him a week. Then he had rushed out of the building and hidden in the forest by the lake.

There had been many close calls, more than he would have liked to admit. Once, a guard had even unknowingly chased him into the lake. After a day of lying around and resting his leg, he had decided that there was no better place for him to be than Silver's office, at the heart of everything.

Yes, it was entirely made of glass and would, therefore, be a lot harder to sneak into. But he started planning.

He soon managed to sneak an unsuspecting human into Ordenia, and used him to distract the guards by embedding a Memory Orb into him, convincing him that Ordenia was actually his homeland.

He reminded himself of the werewolf code they followed in Ordenia: all humans were to be left alone and subjected to magic only in absolute emergency situations. If this wasn't an emergency, Advik didn't know what was.

While the guards sat in a circle around this blabbering human, trying to convince him that this was not indeed a small town in Tanzania and panicking about how he entered Ordenia in the first place, Advik had sprinted across to Silver's office door, stifling a laugh.

The door had a pin code. Advik cursed. What now? An idea occurred to him, and he made his way into Headquarters, sneaking into the staff room and then into the interrogation room. He peeked under the door. It was empty. He put on a coat and gloves in the uniform room next to it. Heart racing, he grabbed a few sleek tools. Then he ran his hands through his hair, messing them up, and grabbed a pair of glasses. Slackening his posture, he made his way back to the glass door.

"The president wants me to sterilize his office," he said to the guards listening raptly to the still-talking human.

"Yes, yes," one of them said impatiently, and in his haste, did not notice Advik watching him punch in the code. 050907. Kiara's birthday. It hurt to be reminded that the man behind so much destruction, so much pain, was his friend's father. A man he'd known, even looked up to, for as long as he could remember.

Fighting the lump in his throat, he thanked the guard and hurriedly stepped through the door.

It had been three days since then. He had quickly managed to locate a broom cupboard inside the office building and was hiding in there. Since it was all made of glass, sneaking around was that much more difficult. He would hide in the broom cupboard all day, sleeping in a small corner. It was awfully constrained, but late at night when everyone was asleep, he would crawl out to explore.

He couldn't risk using a flashlight for the fear of being found out. Instead, he relied on his wolf eyesight and instincts to guide him. He took mental pictures of the things he saw. One night, he managed to find blueprints of every inch of Ordenia in a cleverly hidden drawer. Secret passages even he didn't know of, barricaded routes marked 'X', every office, every room, labelled with the occupant's name. There were certain entries and gateways marked with red, and numbers like 40 or 30 were scrawled next to them. It wouldn't have been easy to obtain these documents, that was for sure.

And that was how Advik found out about the war being waged on Ordenia. On his fourth day in the cupboard, he dressed his healing wound and, at 5:30 p.m., when he knew the guards would disappear for their evening snacks and tea, crept out slowly.

His legs ached from lack of use and he bit back a sigh of relief at being able to walk again. He triumphantly looked up at the security cameras he'd successfully blocked, but the smirk disappeared as suddenly as it had bloomed on his face when he looked out of a window.

He thought his eyes were playing tricks on him. Every direction he turned, he could see people fighting, blood flowing. What was happening? Were his friends out there too? In his worry, he nearly knocked over a vase but caught it at the last second, yet the reverberating bang echoed through the empty office. He swore and ran behind a wall, expecting to see a guard's neck snap up to check. When no one came, he felt his unease grow.

He glanced down at the regular post of the guards. It was deserted. That's when it occurred to him: the guards had joined in the battle. Advik looked out over the glittering lakeside and watched the battle coalesce.

His confusion grew as the opposition drew ranks. Really, what was happening?

Then in the distance, he saw, as if in a dream, Manohar Sharma step forward, the tall figure of Kiara unconscious in his arms. A few men followed him, carrying Amara and Krish. Aidan appeared last, but conscious. There were gaping holes in his t-shirt, and Advik noticed with a jolt that his stomach was heavily bandaged, and he was evidently having trouble standing straight. A lot of Manohar's followers banded behind him, and horror pooled in Advik's stomach as the familiar figure of his former friend, Aisha, joined the ranks.

She seemed to have lost a lot of weight. There was a prominent gash along her cheekbone. Losing all sense of rationality, Advik found himself running across the corridor to the stairway. He had barely taken five steps when the stitch in his leg caught, and he sank to the floor.

A scream of pain and frustration clawed its way out of his throat as he lay on the floor, looking outside the windows helplessly.

36

"THERE, KIA. JUST open your eyes, sweetheart."

Kiara felt her eyes open to her father's concerned face, his familiar voice, and foolishly thought she was in her old bedroom, twelve years old once again, cribbing about being woken up too early for school.

"Papa," she whispered.

"There she is," he whispered back.

"Where–where am I?" she asked. Her head throbbed as everything came flooding back. Her eyes roved over the surroundings, and she suddenly opened her mouth to scream, "AIDAN!"

"He's okay," Manohar reassured her, "He's okay, Kia."

"Papa," she said again, and his eyes softened. "I don't trust you. I can't trust you. I need to see him."

His eyes flickered with emotion for a second, just a second. "Very well, then. Smith, if you will."

"Speak," growled an unfamiliar voice, then, "Kiara, I'm here. I'm okay, love." His voice filled her ears, and Kiara staggered to her feet.

It was now that she properly took in everything around her. Rows and rows of who she could only assume were werewolves were standing around them. With an unpleasant clench in her stomach, she spotted Aisha not far behind. Aidan, Krish and

Amara were surrounded by guards. Amara looked admittedly better. Kiara locked eyes with Aidan, and gratitude and love bloomed inside her. And there he was, Krish, her best friend, her true soulmate. He brought out a smile in her that she wasn't sure she had the capacity for anymore.

"Anjali," boomed Manohar's voice, and the name shocked her back to reality. For there, on the other side, stood an almost equally large army, her mother at its head. "You have all fought gallantly, sacrificed many brilliant, brave soldiers. But surely, even one as innately idealistic as you can see that you have lost. Surrender now, Anjali. Your one last hope–your Elixir–is ours. And even if it was in your possession, the one Katrol you had–our daughter–is one no more. Her trial, for lack of a better word, cleansed her and destroyed her powers. It is futile ..."

Her father kept talking, but his words were only white noise for Kiara now. Something else had entered the forefront of her mind. Her head tilted back slightly as she got sucked into another Memory Orb. This time from–Aisha?

Her own words reverberated through the room, over and over again. *"I forgive you, Aish. Hritik never would have."*

Kiara watched as she left the room with Aidan and Amara. She watched as Aisha's face contorted and she broke down into bitter, broken sobs. For how long the girl continued to cry, Kiara had no idea. She saw into Aisha's mind.

Hritik's funeral–his parents in all white, Rishika likewise, standing next to them. His mother sobbing openly into her husband's chest, with him looking unusually sombre. Advik and Krish watching their friend's body burn, silent tears trickling down their faces, Aisha next to them.

Kiara sensed the sharp pain that Aisha felt for Kiara, pain that pierced her white rage. Kiara, who should have been there next to them. Kiara, who would never be able to outlive her grief. Kiara, one of her oldest friends. Kiara, who despite everything, she loved.

She had let her bitterness and wrath take over. Kiara knew that Aisha was not a bad person, she was merely misguided.

Kiara saw the attack happen the day she left. She saw Smith break into the interrogation room to bust Aisha out of those chains. She saw Aisha sagging against him as he escorted her out of the room, to a large hall where, apparently, a briefing was taking place.

"The plan of action is simple," Manohar Sharma was saying. "My daughter and her companions have been sent off by my unsuspecting wife on a false mission to retrieve the Elixir. The Elixir, which, as you know, we have been working towards obtaining for decades now.

He kept a warm hand on Farber's shoulder. "William here, working alongside other incredible talents, managed to pull off this massively impressive feat just a couple of months ago. The Elixir is now in our possession. As a precaution, we have also ensured that my daughter, the only Katrol among their ranks, will be nullified by the time of her return, which we are not anticipating for at least a couple of weeks.

"With the Elixir–their last hope of a fighting chance–in our hands, we shall offer them an ultimatum. They must surrender, logically, for our army is far superior even without the employment of the Elixir. With it, we are indestructible. For even the threat of the Elixir will make them cower. Victory will, at last, be ours."

Kiara was going to be nullified? Her Katrol powers, the real reason behind Hritik's death, would be destroyed? She would be Kiara once again.

Aisha's friend, Kiara. Aisha's friend, whom she had recklessly tried to kill. But Aisha knew her friends. She knew Anjali Sharma. They would never back down. They would go down fighting, and go down they would, because the army Manohar had created was truly invincible.

Unless ... unless she did something about it.

"Listen to me, Kiara," Aisha's voice said in her ears. "I have a plan to create a distraction. All we have to do now is figure out where the Elixir is, and make sure it is kept somewhere near the hospital wing, so I can quietly slip it into my pocket on my way back. I'm going to have to ingest it. As soon as I do, I want you to run as fast as you can. I bandaged your chest with a lot more layers than were necessary. I have concealed something in there, and with it lies your survival and the elimination of this hideous army. Please let me do this. I failed Hritik once. I don't want that to happen again."

Kiara snapped back to reality. Her heart ached for Aisha. Perhaps it was because she could so closely relate to the other girl's situation that she had to respect her decision.

She sent back a message to Aisha. *Let me talk to my father. I want you to trust me with the Elixir before you have it. Just let me try. I promise to let you carry on and obey your every command if it doesn't work.*

She knew that the Elixir was in President Silver's office. She saw the shimmering reflection of its glass walls in the lake's surface just a few feet away from her.

And through the windows, a figure watched this procession. A figure in a grey t-shirt and blue jeans.

Kiara's heart skipped a beat. *Advik?*

It made no sense, yet it was the only possible explanation. A conversation with Krish came to her mind.

"So can I just do this to anyone?" she asked.

"As long as they're in your line of sight," he replied.

She closed her eyes as she began constructing, for the second time today, and the third time in her life, a message from her own memory.

37

ADVIK FELT A funny sensation sneak up on him.

His head rolled backwards and Kiara's strong voice filled his ears.

Advik, *it said,* I'm at the lakeside right now. I can see your reflection in the water. Papa let slip that the Elixir is in Silver's office. I don't have much time to explain, but I need you to find it and get it to the hospital wing in exactly ten minutes. And in case something ... happens to me, thank you. For everything.

Advik wiped the sweat on his face and carefully stood up. Silver had many rooms in this building, but there was one in particular which was his personal office. Throwing open the door, he began searching frantically. He ruffled through all the desks, drawers and cupboards in search of a safe, but found none. He kept checking his watch every couple of seconds, watching the time pass away.

He could find absolutely nothing. His brain was shockingly, frustratingly empty. His leg was killing him. He reached the door and twisted the knob, about to go out and send a message to Kiara saying that he'd tried, that he couldn't do it, when he noticed Silver's black overcoat hanging by gleaming, silver hooks screwed at the back of the door. He knew it was a desperate, probably ridiculous idea. But he was out of time, out of options.

His fumbling fingers reached inside the left pocket. It was empty, save for a few candy wrappers and some spare cash. He reached into the other pocket, and felt his palm wrap around what felt like a small vial.

His heart stilled. Hardly daring to breathe, he pulled his hand out.

There, enclosed in his fist, gleaming in the sunlight, was a tiny bottle. The weather-worn, age-old label read, in a stunning cursive font, "ELIXIR".

38

AMARA LISTENED TO Manohar Sharma's garbage impatiently.

Her fingers twitched in anxiety. She kept telling herself to breathe. After having received proper medical and magical treatment, she had gotten back on her feet. She had also eaten her first real meal in days.

Now, Aisha stood in front of her, her slight, elegant figure achingly familiar. Having been friends ever since Aisha had Turned, it was a punch in the gut to realize she'd been double crossing them the whole time. Yet, when she flipped her hair back and nodded at Amara, Amara followed the instructions the Orb had conveyed. She gradually increased the speed and volume of her breathing to a near-concerning level.

"Can't ... breathe," she rasped, as if out of breath. Krish, who was completely unaware of the scheme, called out for help. At that precise moment, Amara swooned and pretended to faint on the spot. Unrest rippled through the gathered ensemble.

Even Manohar Sharma stopped speaking to enquire about the cause of the disturbance. "Someone get a medic," he said through gritted teeth.

"Allow me," Aisha chirped, and Amara opened her eyes a smidge to see the other girl throw her a small, almost imperceptible, wink.

"... and our agenda includes ..." Kiara's father was saying, when she felt something small and cold slip into her palm. With the expertise of a pickpocket, Aisha melted into the crowd.

"Enough," Kiara said, the word getting stuck in her throat. She stepped forward to stand at her father's level. "Enough," she repeated, in a stronger, more commanding voice.

She strode ahead and turned to face her father and his army. Surprise flickered across her father's face. His lips parted. He blinked slowly, then seemed to regain his composure.

He chuckled. "What are you doing, child? What is the meaning of this?"

Without a moment's hesitation, Kiara thrust her fist upwards to showcase the shimmering bottle to both sides present. A wave of satisfaction hit her as she registered sheer unbridled shock on her father's normally composed profile.

"This," she said, feeling her resolve strengthen, "is the only real weapon–the only real threat you have against us. Sure, our numbers have dwindled, and yes, you are Katrols." She paused for a second, marvelling at her own words. *You* are Katrols. "But your numbers have diminished too. And without this, we have a fighting chance. I can so easily just–" Kiara deliberately dropped the bottle and caught it again, drawing a collective gasp from the gathered crowd.

"I have some conditions," she said, shrugging noncommittally. "I am not unreasonable. First, and most urgently, release my friends to the other side."

Her own glare challenged her father's. He relented first, of course he did.

"Send the children forward," he ordered.

Amara 'regained consciousness' as she joined a shocked Krish and a staggering Aidan, not only to the front of the gathering, but even further, past Kiara, into Anjali's ranks. She felt Aidan's palm lightly graze her arm as he passed her.

"I want you to let them go back indoors and return to safety right now. They won't be a threat to you any longer. It's just me now. Me and this," she tipped the Elixir, "tiny ... little ... bottle."

Kiara turned to her mother, who looked very disturbed and reluctant. She mouthed, "Trust me, please."

Though Anjali looked displeased, she didn't protest. Her jaw hardened but her eyes gleamed with tears and pride.

"Done," her father growled.

Kiara lifted the heel of her shoe and carefully placed the bottle under her foot. "I'm going to watch as every last one of them leaves. If even one of you makes a move towards me when my back is turned, I can put my foot down in a second." She loathed the half-impressed look on her father's face.

She watched as one by one, the army, her army, turned on their heels and trudged into the Headquarters or into their own residential spaces. Aidan, Krish and Amara lingered the longest.

"I love you," she mouthed at all three of them. "Please go."

Amara nodded with tears in her eyes. She grabbed Krish and Aidan by their arms and steered them inside.

"Anyone else who doesn't want to stand by this army, anyone else at all who wants to do what's good, what's right, please follow them. Follow my friends."

Kiara looked to the army, and was surprised to see not one of them flinching in their resolve. Her father didn't even blink at their unwavering loyalty and surety.

At her questioning look, he replied, "This is a family. We would rather die together than run away like cowards."

Kiara took a deep breath. The way he conducted the army, the way he led all of them–no wonder they'd made it this far. They could not be allowed to go any further.

"I want you and your army to retreat right now. To turn around and walk out the door, leaving any and all of the possessions you may have, here. I want you to leave. I want each of you to consume a memory-altering potion, closely supervised by us, to erase any memories you have of Ordenia. Once that is done, you will go back to wherever you emerged from, and start your own little sect of werewolves. I want you to walk out and never return. To start a new life and live it to its fullest. I want your army, and all traces of your army, to leave Ordenia forever. I want you to forfeit your messed up, violent, disgusting dream."

For a few moments, she watched the battle on her father's face as he turned over her words. Was he considering them?

"Kia–" he began, as Kiara felt her heart sink. She knew that tone. It was the one he used when he was disappointed. The one he used when he was going to say a flat-out "no".

"I can't do that, sweetheart," he said, and the sincerity of his words, the familiarity of his voice almost broke her. Almost. Kiara closed her eyes in resignation.

"Aisha," she choked on the word, as if forcing herself to say it. Quick as lightning, Aisha was at her side.

"Hritik would be proud of you," Kiara murmured as she hugged her friend.

A single tear slipped out of Aisha's eye. "Go, Kiara. Run."

And so, she did. She ran past the army of Katrols, past her father, past the life she could've had, past the friend she had thought she'd lost. She didn't look back to see Aisha unstopper the bottle. She didn't look back to see her drain it of the very last drop. She didn't look back to see her finally, truly, gone. She didn't realize that that was the last time she'd see her father, too.

Kiara ran as far as she could into the depths of the forest. She hastily took off her shirt and unravelled the bandages underneath. She found a tiny, gleaming silver gun, barely bigger than the palm of her hand. A single silver bullet was taped across its front. With trembling fingers, she loaded the gun. She put her shirt back on and held the gun so tightly it hurt.

And then, with bated breath, she waited. And waited. And waited.

And it didn't matter how far away she was. There was no way she could've missed the sound of a monster, of a killer. The shrieks and cries she'd heard that day would haunt her for a long time to come. She heard people trying to run, to escape. As every shrill cry, every sob stabbed at her heart, she reminded herself that she'd given them a chance to leave, a chance to live.

She tried hardest of all to drown out the growls of the wolf. She didn't know how long she waited. Minutes (or was it hours?) slipped by her until ...

The hairs on the back of her head stood up. She heard the heavy breathing of a wolf. The low, guttural growling jolted her body, putting every inch on alert. She slowly crept out of the bushes that she was hiding behind.

And then Kiara saw it—a wolf in light grey fur. It was a hundred metres from her, and it was gaining speed. Closing the distance. As it flew towards her, she tried frantically to look for a sign of her old friend, a glimmer of hope. She found none. Its eyes were red and ravenous. Any flicker of humanity was gone.

And that, finally, was the last straw.

She raised the gun and closed her eyes. "I hope you find peace, Aish," she whispered, and pulled the trigger.

39

"YOU'RE FREE TO go, Ms Sharma," said the lady in the white lab coat.

Kiara jumped out of the hospital bed so quickly one would assume she'd received an electric shock. She ran out of the room at an alarming speed, wanting nothing more than to get to the residential area and find–

Aidan was asleep on a bench right opposite the room she was in. Her obnoxiously loud footsteps seemed to have awoken him. His eyes fluttered open and he wiped at the drool on his chin.

"Kiara," he whispered, his voice hoarse.

Kiara had come out of that room desperate to know what had happened after she'd passed out in the woods. But there would be plenty of time to talk later.

She sprinted ahead and threw herself into Aidan's lap. He caught her, his hand warm and solid on her back. His head was on her shoulder, her fingers running through his hair.

He pulled away first. "Are you okay? We saw what happened."

Of course. They had had to clean it all up.

She shook her head slightly. "Are you?"

He didn't answer, but she knew. They weren't okay, wouldn't be for a long time to come. Aidan's bruised fingers traced her lips. She looked straight into his blue-green eyes as she closed the distance between them.

Whenever Kiara had imagined kissing him in the last few weeks, she had always pictured it as this desperate, passionate, fiery thing, like the first time in her room. But when they locked lips, it was gentle, sweet and beautifully slow, for it was a promise.

A promise for now and the future.

Epilogue

Five years later

KIARA GLOWED WITH pride as Alicia awoke.

"Congratulations," she said. "You're no longer a Katrol." Tears shone in the eighteen-year-old's eyes as she hugged Kiara tightly.

"Thank you," she whispered. Kiara just held her tight.

It was late, but Kiara decided to assist the medics for another ten minutes before taking her leave. Aidan was cooking tonight. While walking back to the beautiful lakeside house they'd recently moved into, she bumped into Amara, also on her way back from work. Krish and Amara had recently gotten engaged and moved in together.

"You just got off?" Kiara inquired.

"It was a long day. I'm sure Aidan will fill you in." As tired as Amara looked, the pride and satisfaction in her voice was obvious. "Are you going for your session tomorrow?"

Kiara nodded.

"Then we'll see you there," Amara said, kissing her on the cheek.

The five of them–Kiara, Amara, Aidan, Advik and Krish–had been attending group therapy for almost five years. It had been a godsend for all of them as they attempted to heal and move on from their ordeal five years ago.

"Give Krish my love," Kiara said.

"You guys literally hung out two hours ago!" Amara laughed.

Kiara smiled. Her love for her best friend would always outweigh everything else.

"He's walking the dogs right now, but I'll tell him when he's home. I'm sure you'll see him soon anyway," Amara said.

They waved goodbye, and Kiara turned her head to the identical house where Advik lived with his girlfriend, Alexa. Alexa was appointed to look after Advik, to guide him through his physical therapy. Somewhere along the way, spending so many hours and days together, the two had fallen in love and became inseparable ever since.

Feeling ravenous by now, Kiara walked into the gorgeous, cozy home she'd shared with Aidan for what seemed like forever. Aidan's warm, strong embrace greeted her in the kitchen. He smelled of cinnamon.

"Hi, love," he whispered in her ear.

"Long day?" she asked, cupping his face in her hands.

"Mm-hmm," he replied, eyes shuttering close at her touch.

"You and me both. Wanna ditch the table and eat in bed?"

"Now there's an idea."

Aidan's arm was around her as they ate, as warm and comfortable as her favourite hoodie. She smiled. "Tell me about your day."

"It was exhausting," he admitted. "But so, so rewarding."

As he launched into his narrative, she thought about how Amara had approached him about it for the first time. "Manohar Sharma did heinous, unforgivable things," she had said, and even through her grief, Kiara had agreed. "Ordenia needs to be more welcoming, more inclusive to the diverse range of people it houses and will continue to house in the future. The last thing we want is for someone to feel excluded because of, or be ashamed, of their ethnicity, sexuality, disability or race; we've been silent and tolerant for too long."

And so, their organization was born. They had recruited Advik as well, and the three of them were a force to be reckoned with.

"That's incredible," Kiara said when Aidan was finished. "I'm so proud of you."

Aidan blushed. "How's Alicia?"

Kiara beamed with pride. "Our third official transformation."

While it had been brutal and barbaric, the protection Kiara's father had employed for the faux Elixir had rid her of her fire. She had guessed that some form of the same experiment had been used to tame his army all those years ago. She had taken up from there and worked tirelessly for three years, along with researchers and scientists, to come up with a lot less dangerous and traumatizing, but equally accurate and effective way to rid a Katrol of their fire.

A large team in their organization worked on scouting Katrols from different parts of the world and helping them convert and rehabilitate.

Aidan's face lit up. "That's ... wow, that's incredible, Kiara."

As her eyes swept over his smiling face, his shining eyes, she couldn't help but think of how lucky she was that her father had Turned her.

She fell asleep on his shoulder that night.

A blissful, dreamless slumber.

Acknowledgements

THANK YOU TO my incredible parents, Sonika and Gautam Chopra for being the pillars of support they have been. I truly could not have done this without you.

Thank you to the rest of my incredible extended family. I am so lucky to be born into a family of lifelong cheerleaders.

Thank you to my amazing friends for being nothing but excited and happy for me. You guys are my chosen family.

Lastly, I would like to thank Mr Omung Kumar for his phenomenal artwork that you can see on the cover page and throughout this book. Your talent and enthusiasm is more than I could ever have hoped for.

About the Author

Shannaaya Chopra is a 19-year-old college student, currently pursuing a degree in psychology. Born and brought up in Mumbai, she considers the city her forever home. She has been a voracious reader ever since she gained the ability to read, which eventually morphed into a great love for writing as well. She has a dog named Happy and a little sister who she calls Tiny. They are more precious to her than anything in the world. Shannaaya enjoys playing badminton, swimming and (though she can never learn the choreography) dancing with her friends. She hopes that *The Turning* is just the beginning of a very long line of books to come.

About the Illustrator

Omung Kumar, the illustrator of the book, is a National Award-winning film director, acclaimed for powerful biopics like *Mary Kom* and *Sarbjit.* He is a passionate art enthusiast known for creating mind-blowing paintings and designing mesmerizing sets for movies, major events and TV shows where his artistic vision brings grand spectacles to life.

HarperCollins *Publishers* India

At HarperCollins India, we believe in telling the best stories and finding the widest readership for our books in every format possible. We started publishing in 1992; a great deal has changed since then, but what has remained constant is the passion with which our authors write their books, the love with which readers receive them, and the sheer joy and excitement that we as publishers feel in being a part of the publishing process.

Over the years, we've had the pleasure of publishing some of the finest writing from the subcontinent and around the world, including several award-winning titles and some of the biggest bestsellers in India's publishing history. But nothing has meant more to us than the fact that millions of people have read the books we published, and that somewhere, a book of ours might have made a difference.

As we look to the future, we go back to that one word—a word which has been a driving force for us all these years.

Read.